London Calling

Chelsea Bee

Text copyright © 2017 Chelsea Beaton.
Cover art copyright © 2017 Tara Thompson.

All rights reserved. No part of this document may be reproduced or transmitted in any form or by any means, electronic, mechanical, photocopying, recording, or otherwise, without prior written permission of Chelsea Beaton.

This work is a work of the author's imagination. Any resemblance to any person(s), living or dead, is entirely coincidental. Any reference to organizations or businesses mentioned in this work does not represent the organization or business, and is not meant to defame any person, organization, or business.

Print ISBN: 1548168343
Print ISBN - 13: 978-15481638346

Fools and Mortals Press
St. John's

a novel

Chelsea Bee

Fools and Mortals Press

This book is dedicated to every woman who has been impacted in some way by sexual assault.
I believe you.
I support you.
I love you.

It was not your fault.

10% of the proceeds from this book will go to support survivors of sexual violence.

Prologue

Hell is empty and all the devils are here -
The Tempest, William Shakespeare

I try to hide in the closet at the top of the stairs as I hear my Mom call out to me. My knees are up by my chin, and my long arms are wrapped around my shins.

"Olivia, where are you? There you are, what in the name of God are you hiding in the closet for?" Mom asks when she opens the closet door, "come on down Aunt Jackie and Michael are here."

I reluctantly take her hand and follow her down the stairs. Michael stands tall in front of me, he's grown since I've seen him last. We only see each other for one weekend every year, and it's always the worst weekend of the year.

He smacks his gum around in his mouth and blows a pathetic bubble. His face is spotted with zits and I can see the oil pockets in his pores. I hope that my teenage years are at least a little kinder to me than they are to him.

"Olivia, show Michael to his room, please," my Mother says, looking pointedly at me. I'm not sure why she wants me to show him to his room. He's been here before and the spare bedroom hasn't moved. Besides, I'm only nine, playing hostess to my evil aunt and her even more evil son wasn't my idea. I remember Mom is making my favourite dessert tonight, and if I embarrass her in front of her sister by being rude I won't be able to have any, so I take Michael up the stairs.

"What's got you in such a bad mood?"

"You. I was supposed to go to Cassandra's birthday party but Mom said I have to be here while you're here."

"Don't worry, we can have more fun by ."

I take his things up to the spare bedroom and his Mom takes the pullout bed. We used to share a room until a few years ago and our Moms decided we were too old for that.

I can smell the ham cooking in the oven and hope dinner is ready soon. Mom made my favourite, ham with mashed potatoes and black raspberry cake with cherries on top. We sit down at the dining table we only use for fancy occasions, with the food spread out in front of us. Mom is on her third glass of wine, she always drinks a little more wine when Aunt Jackie is here. I reach for the mashed potato spoon before Mom stops me.

"Now, Olivia, please let Michael take up his dinner first," my Dad says.

I recoil my arm and wait until Jackie and Michael finish getting their meals. I love ham with pineapple and mashed potatoes, except this dinner is ruined by Michael chomping on his food with his mouth open from the other side of the room. My little brother, John, has already finished his food and left to go play with his friends. I think he's half boy, half vacuum cleaner by the way he eats. I realize my face is showing how annoyed I am when my Dad looks at me and clears his throat. I try to smile.

"Now, everyone will have to excuse me. I see someone has gotten in to the cake," my Mom looks at Michael. I know exactly which piece of the cake I want. I want one of the corner pieces with at least one cherry. As many cherries as possible is ideal, though. Before I can get close to it, Mom puts the cake down in front of Michael and he scoops the only remaining corner piece on to his plate. Apparently he ate the other three corners earlier. He picks up his spoon and runs it along the top of the cake, shaving off most of the icing and all of the remaining cherries. He shrugs, like there was nothing he could do but eat half of it.

"Oh, Michael," his Mom says, though makes no move to scold him.

"Do you want a piece, Olivia?" My Dad asks.

"No thanks. I'm fine." I scowl and get up from the table.

~ ~ ~

I hear my bedroom door creak open and my stomach feels like it's sitting in my chest.

"Don't scream. Don't say anything," I hear a boy's voice whisper from the doorway.

"Michael?" I ask.

"Yeah, it's me. I couldn't sleep. I had a bad dream. Can I sleep with you?"

"Why don't you go in your Mom's room?"

"She's sleeping on the couch, I don't want to. Just let me sleep with you," he says, slowly approaching my bed.

"You can sleep on the floor." I put my arm out on my bed to keep him from lying down next to me.

"No, that's not comfortable. Just let me in." He moves my arm back to my side and slides in to the bed.

"Now go to sleep." I roll over to turn my back to him.

I can feel him breathing on my neck. I flinch when he puts his hand on my thigh.

"Don't move. Don't say anything," he whispers in my ear.

"I'll scream," I try to say in a threatening voice, cracking at the end.

"I'll tell your Mom you want it. She'll believe me."

"No she won't."

"She will. She didn't believe you when you I broke her favourite lamp last year. What's the difference? She'll ground you now like she did back then."

He's right. I was grounded for a week because Michael broke the expensive lamp.

He puts his hand under my pyjama pants and I try not to think about what he's doing.

Chapter One

Do not be afraid of greatness. Some are born great, some achieve greatness, and others have greatness trust upon them - Twelfth Night, William Shakespeare

    I sit in my Shakespeare class as the professor is handing back the graded papers. He looks at me and asks if he can see me after class is finished. *Is my term paper on the Globe Theatre really that bad?* I sit there waiting for the other students to file out before approaching his desk.
    "Olivia. How are you?" Professor Jones greets me. He doesn't seem mad. Maybe it's not *that* bad after all.

"I'm well," I say, biting my nails as usual.

"I really enjoyed your paper. You seem to have a real love and admiration for his work," he says, pulling a sheet of paper from his briefcase.

"I love it," I say, "I think his plays are so beautiful." Huh. I guess it's not that bad.

"There's this program I think you might be interested in. The Globe has a summer program for performing arts students every year. It's a three month stay. It's not cheap, there are scholarships available though. I really think this could be a good fit for you." He hands me a shiny poster with a photo of the parliament buildings against a light blue sky. The poster advertises "Learn - Work - Live". I take it. A professor thinks I can perform in London. It's hard to believe. He's studied Shakespeare for most of his career, and he really thinks I can perform at the Globe.

"Thank you," I take it, "you really think I can get in to this program?"

"I think you're one of my most promising first year students. And from what I hear about your acting, you have talent there, too. You'll need a reference for the application and I would be more than happy to provide one. Think about it, discuss it with your parents if you have to. Let me know by Monday if you want the reference. This is a great opportunity, I would really consider taking it. Travelling is one of the best learning experiences you'll have in university. And if you need any more reason to do it, they have you take academic classes that are easily transferred, so you'll be given university credits for the work you do," he says.

"Thanks again," I say and walk out in to the hallway and start making my way back to my dorm room.

I'll have to take up extra shifts at work. They're always looking to fill hours at the restaurant, and there are probably about ten hours a week I can use to work instead of my usual run or reading. I can make it work. I get back to my room and log on to the website to see the program details. It's expensive. Almost five thousand dollars, not including spending money. Mom and Dad are having a hard time paying for my schooling already, which made me take out a loan last year. I'll never be able to save up for the program fee. The program is amazing. A dream come true. There will be a production of a play yet to be announced, and the website boasts the program is a great introduction to the theatre world. A contract will be given to the most promising student at the end of the term. Plus, it will look amazing on a resume.

I *need* to do this. The chances of me getting in are slim, still I have to at least try. I'll get the scholarship. I'll make sure of it.

~ ~ ~

"You know you're never going to get in, right?" My best friend and roommate Jenna says.

"Glad to know I have such a supportive friend," I reply, filling my dinner plate with salad. Jenna insists on eating from the salad bar every day. We both promised we would get healthier this year, so I eat the wilted lettuce.

"I mean I would love for you to go, you have to realize that it's so competitive though," she says as I put the best looking bite of spinach in my mouth.

"I know. I'm working really hard, you know that. I've been getting almost straight A's since I started going here, and I've been practically slaving over my audition tape for the past week."

"Keep working at it. Even if you don't get in this year, maybe next."

I put the fork down and decide I'm over the whole salad thing, and go back to the kitchen to get some much needed french fries. I try not to think about the fact that they were being drowned in fat only minutes earlier.

~ ~ ~

I will not take no for an answer for this scholarship. "Hello, my name is Olivia Williams. I'm from Memorial University of Newfoundland, and I wanted to thank you for your time and consideration."

And I rehearse the same monologue from Othello for the two-hundredth and sixth time. I've been counting.

"That I did love the Moor to live with him,
My downright violence and storm of fortunes
May trumpet to the world: my heart's subdued
Even to the very quality of my lord:
I saw Othello's visage in his mind,
And to his honour and his valiant parts
Did I my soul and fortunes consecrate.
So that, dear lords, if I be left behind,
A moth of peace, and he go to the war,
The rites for which I love him are bereft me,

And I a heavy interim shall support
By his dear absence. Let me go with him."

"Knock, knock," I hear someone say from my open doorway.

"Max!" I skip over to the door and give him a hug. How was Norway?"

"Amazing. Cold. Beautiful."

"I'm still so jealous you were able to go."

"I know, you're going to have an amazing time in London though."

"If I get the scholarship. I already got the conditional acceptance. Now it just depends on the fees."

"So make it happen."

"I'm trying. It's competitive."

"Can you take extra shifts at work?"

"Sure, I can take some extra - I can't let my grades slip by working too much though. I'm saving up everything extra I make just in case I do get in, I can have some spending and going out money. And besides, you know that Sally has been having some issues lately that I need to get looked at. She's getting old, she needs some TLC." Sally is my car, a 1993 chilli red mini cooper. I inherited her after Grandma Williams died a year ago. When I inherited her I splurged on a Union Jack decal for the roof. Now I wish I had saved that money for London, or maintenance I know Sally will need soon. I can only turn up the volume on the radio to ignore the rattling in the engine for so long. I need my car to get to and from work from Marlowe's, the fish and chips chain restaurant I've been working as a waitress in. It's hardly enough hours or high enough tips to afford the program fees. I think people are finally realizing how bad and

greasy our food is, so business has slowed in recent months.
"I know you can do it. Oh, I brought these." He opens his book bag and pulls out a box of almost crushed donuts.
"No. Way. Here, I have the movie all set up." Max and I started Movie Night Mondays years ago when my high school boyfriend broke up with me. I called him in the middle of the night late on a Sunday. He stayed with me for a few days when I didn't want to be alone. He's been around ever since.

"That was the worst movie ever," Max says and pops the last piece of chocolate in his mouth. I always let him have the last piece.
"*Grease* is a classic. You can't hate it."
"*Grease* is not a classic," Max says, putting his hand on mine. I feel butterflies erupt in my stomach and make me feel ill.
My phone beeps with a text from Jenna.
Bathroom. SOS.
I laugh and take the box on tampons from my desk to bring to my distressed friend. Max laughs behind me at her misfortune.

~ ~ ~

Today is the day. Today, they are going to call everyone who gets the scholarships. And I'm stuck at work for the occasion. I glance at the clock. 12:37. It's the middle of the lunch time rush, and all of three tables are occupied. Only three tables, and I managed to get the most annoying one. *Of course you got all the tables, Olivia, you're the only waitress in right now. Idiot.*

"Hmmmm, I guess I'll have the pan fried scallops and the poutine on the side."

"Add dressing?" I ask the woman seated in front of me. I gently tap my pen on the small notepad, hoping she hurries up with her order. She's wearing a tie dye sweatshirt with cat faces on it. I'm slightly weirded out, and equally jealous of it.

bzzzzz bzzzz, my phone vibrates in my pocket.

"Uhhhh, I don't know. Honey, should I add dressing?" She asks her husband

bzzzzz bzzzzzz

"No dear, you never like it."

bzzzzz bzzzzzz

"I'm sure I've had it here before."

My heart rate begins to quicken as my phone buzzes its last ring.

bzzzzzzz

I start to sweat as I realize the phone goes silent. I swear to God, if this couple doesn't leave a good tip I'm going to freak out. They probably won't so she can buy more cat sweaters.

"I've heard it's really good here, though," she says to her husband.

Then again, apparently I'm not going to London. I guess I don't need the money. I'll just stay here for the summer. While I'm at it, might as well drop out and work at the restaurant forever. Yeah, I'm sure *that* would be fine. I can't believe this woman didn't let me pick up the fucking phone.

bzzzzz bzzzzzz my phone begins again. And just like that, I feel my spirits lift. Maybe my future isn't doomed to failure.

"Hmmmm…" that God awful woman is still unsure about her order, holy crap.

I peek down at my phone in my apron pocket as she studies the menu. One missed call. United Kingdom. Damnit.

"Order's up," Mildred, my coworker calls out.

bzzzzzzz bzzzzzz "I'll give you a moment to decide," I tell the woman at the table.

I grab the plates of food Mildred has displayed on the pick up area and bring them out to the dining room.

Another customer taps me on my shoulder.

"Hi, ma'am? We're ready for our bill. We were waiting forever for it, you really should hurry up…"

"ENOUGH!" I slam the plates down on a nearby table and march over to Catwoman's table and snatch the menu out of the indecisive woman's hands.

"You," I turn around and face the man who wants his bill. I decide he's going to be called Bill now. He kind of looks like a Bill - is there anyone who is a balding middle aged white man who isn't named Bill? "I'll be with you in a minute. Can't you see I'm busy?" Bill looks taken aback.

"Hello?" I try to say professionally and casually when I answer the phone. I hope they can't tell I'm panicking and that I smell like french fry grease and my hair is oily even though I've only been at work for an hour and I washed my hair this morning. I hear the customers scoff behind me. At this point everyone has turned to see why the waitress is having a meltdown.

"Hello, Olivia. This is Janet from the recruitment office here in the Globe Theatre. We are pleased to inform you that you received the scholarship you applied for. We really hope you'll be able to join us in June," the pleasant voice on the phone says.

"Um, of course I'll be there." It's hard to contain my excitement.

"Fabulous. In a couple of days we'll be mailing you your flight plans and itinerary for the program. We'll see you soon." I hang up the phone and awkwardly try to stop grinning when I realize all the customers are still staring at me.

"Can I speak to your manager?" Bill's wife asks.

"Sure. His name is Tim and he's the creepy as hell one you'll never see here because he's always on a vacation with his nineteen year old girlfriend, so he's in Bora Bora right now, but I can take your name and number and pretend I'll give it to him," I snap at Bill and his wife.

"I'll have the dressing, thanks." Catwoman timidly tells me. She hands the remaining menu back. I offer her a tight lipped smile and return to the kitchen.

"Mildred, I got the scholarship," I nearly squeal it but try to keep my voice down so the handful of customers in the dining room don't realize I was lying about the emergency.

"You got what?"

"A scholarship. Money. Whatever, I get to go to London this summer."

"That's nice, Olivia. Why don't you see if table three needs more water."

~ ~ ~

I nearly break down Jenna's door when I get home.

"The fuck?" She asks, startled.

"I GOT IN, I DID IT!"

"AH, I knew you could!"

No, she didn't, but I think it's best not to mention that. Instead we happy dance in her very pink room. Multi coloured dots line the walls. She has pink satin sheets, a dark pink quilt on her bed, and white and pink picture frames with pictures of the two of us and her high school friends. She even has a pink streak in her shoulder length brown hair.

"This is going to be amazing. I'll let you borrow some of my travel London books." Jenna's Dad is a pilot so she has travelled a lot more than I have. I'm fairly sure she has only read travel books for the last decade.

~ ~ ~

A week later I get my official acceptance letter and itinerary.

June 1, 2014: Check in day for all students

June 5, 2014: Classes commence for all students

August 1, 2014: Classes cease for all students

August 5-10, 2014: Final examinations

August 15, 2014: Performance and giving of awards

August 30, 2014: Check out date for all students

I open the lid to my laptop to look up the Globe on google street view. I type in "The Globe Theatre, London, England" and watch the globe spin and zoom in until it finds the right spot. My screen is filled with a white bubble shaped building. There's a large red sign that shows the schedule of performances for the productions. There are a number of blurred tourists and business people passing by. I navigate around the screen and see bars and coffee shops lining the roads of the Thames. There are even tall apartment buildings with a view of the river. What I wouldn't give to live in one of those. It's hard to believe that I have the opportunity to see this every day.

~ ~ ~

"You need to leave this room, you're never going to get anything packed in this mess," Jenna says when she comes in my room and sees the state of my room. I look around like it's the first time I've seen the fallen stack of books across the floor and the mounds of cloths surrounding me.

"Go get in the shower. We're going out. And while you're doing that I'm cleaning this up and packing for you. You know I won't be able to sleep tonight knowing this place is a mess." She's right. The only reason our rooms ever look presentable is because of her and her need to have things nice and neat, and I do as I'm told. There's no use in arguing with her at this point.

When I get out of the shower and dry my hair I decide to put on some makeup as well. I don't wear it very often but putting it on helps me de-stress a little sometimes. I carefully cover the imperfections on my face with pale toned foundation. I dab pink powder on the apples of my cheeks. I decide to keep it simple and only cover my eyelashes in mascara, and put on a light pink lipstick.

"There we go." Jenna zips up my suitcase when I return to my room, "You look nice. Also, you don't need to bring a thousand books with you for the summer. You can bring one, maybe two for the plane. That's it. They have bookstores in London, Sweetie," taking one, maybe two books? The thought makes me nervous. Still, I know it's never a good idea to argue with her. She's a pre-law major and a shoo in for any school of her choice. I'm not going to win this argument.

"Now, we're going for margaritas and tacos. Max and Steven are on their way. You know I can't let you leave me for the summer without drinks first." A couple drinks might not be such a bad idea.

"Can you curl my hair?" Jenna asks me.

I get the curling wand out of my dresser drawer and begin heating it up.

"So what do you want to do while you're there?" She asks.

"Everything. Anything," I say, "I should look at campuses for when I finally figure out what I want to do with my life and apply to a grad school, and you can apply to a law school in England. We'll go together," I suggest.

"Oh, I wish. No, Steven would never be cool with that."

"Can't you come for like a year?"

"You know what he's like. He's so needy," she says.

"I hate boys."

"You mean everyone except Max."

"Maybe."

Just as we finish, I hear a knock at the door. Max and Steven are here. I feel butterflies when I think about him and wish he was there just to pick me up to go out on a date. I hope he's wearing the blue flannel shirt I love and that he wears three days a week. I realize that I'm probably paying too much attention to what he's wearing, but I love that shirt. Just once I would like to think of him as a normal friend. I know he would never go for me and I have to get over that. He had his chances to date me and never took it. Over the years I've seen girlfriends of his come and go. I pepped him up before the first dates and comforted him after they ended.

We kissed once. I thought that was the moment he would see me as more than a friend, but it didn't happen that way.

It was last year. We're sitting in Jenna's room with as many of our friends as we can squeeze in to the tiny space. We're sitting on her bed with our backs to the wall, everyone else sitting in front of us. His arm has been around my waist for the last hour, and I can hardly focus on the movie. I feel like I'm in middle school going through my first crush all over again. As the movie comes to an end, he carefully turns my face and kisses me gently. He smells like spearmint and Tom Ford Noir. Jenna is the only one who notices what happened and immediately texts me.

Oh my god! Is he staying over?

No, he won't be. It was just once.

The movie ends and he gives my hand a quick squeeze before heading out.

"So are we going to talk about this?" Jenna asks as everyone else slowly trickles out.

"No, probably not. It was just once. Soon he'll realize he's too hot for me and all will be right in the world again."

"You need to fuck him," she says.

"I need to get some water."

I take my water bottle off my desk, slip on my fuzzy bunny slippers, and go in to the kitchen. My heart sinks when I see them there.

Max and Stacey are making out in the kitchen. They dated last year but they broke up when she cheated on him, but I always suspected they still had a thing for each other. Apparently I was right. She has him pinned against the wall in a corner of the room, probably to keep people seeing them while walking by. I stare at them in disbelief before running back to my room.

"Olivia, wait," I hear Max call from behind me as I open my door. I quickly slam it shut.

Bang.

My phone buzzes in my pocket.

It wasn't what it looked like. She came on to me, I swear.

So what are we now? I ask. I'm not sure what kind of a reply I want. For him to apologize? He probably wouldn't mean it. But I still need to hear it from him.

Just friends. We just kissed once. I really like you, but I'm not ready for a relationship yet. Maybe later, just give me some time. And Stacey was just a one time thing, I swear.

So I believe him. I just let everything happen like it normally would, and hope he will come around. I like being single, too. I just think I would like being with him a little more.

~ ~ ~

The night goes by as it usually does. Jenna and Steven have been together for over a year at this point so I'm used to it being the four of us. It's easy to forget sometimes that Max and I aren't together, he's just Steven's best friend.

"Hey, do you want to come over for a little bit?" Max asks while we're paying our bills. Jenna and Steven are already waiting for us by the door. The woman at the front of the restaurant winks at me when he says it. *Why would she make this more awkward than it needs to be?*

"You know I live really close by and I thought we could go for a little walk home. And maybe, you know, watch a movie or something. So we can hang out more before you go. It's only three days away, we don't have too much time left together," he says.

"Yeah, of course. Just let me tell Jenna I'm not coming home with her." I cross the room and look at Jenna and Steven. Steven knows that look. That is a We Need Girl Talk So Please Leave Look. He does.

"I'm not coming home," I say.

"Oh. My. God. Good luck. And Let me know if you need a ride home in the morning. His place is too far to walk back to campus."

I leave the restaurant and Max is waiting outside. We begin walking while Jenna and Steven are waiting for their taxi to get here.

"So, are you excited to leave?" Max asks me.

"Yeah I am. I'm nervous to leave and know I'm going to miss home a lot but still this is something I've dreamed of for years."

"What do you have planned?"

"A lot. I hope I have time to do it all. I want to see everything the Globe puts off. I'll be there so I have to take that kind of an opportunity. Maybe I can see something in the Piccadilly theatre – I haven't bought tickets yet though, I'll have to see what's playing – I want to go on the London Eye and see as much of the city as possible.

"I wish I could have gone with you," he says when we approach his front door "I'm really going to miss you." He starts leaning closer to me. I quickly panic and wonder if my breath still smells acceptable. It probably smells like lime, tequila, and taco beef.

Instead of kissing me he just opens the door and gestures for me to go in. His roommates are sleeping so we try to get into his room quietly.

"You know, you're beautiful," he says as he takes me by the waist. "I really don't want you to go. I've had feelings for you for a long time." I'm speechless. He picks right now to tell me this? Right before I'm supposed to leave the country? His lips reach my neck. I think It's slightly weird that he waited until days before I leave but I'm not about to complain now. I wrap my arms around his neck and pull him closer.

He pushes me on to the bed. We're moving faster than I would have liked but I've been waiting years for this. I'm ready. I run my hands through his dark blonde hair and bite him on the lip slightly. He moans and reaches under my shirt. It's not that big of a deal, I've had sex before. I hope this will only help him to see me as someone he could consider being with long term. The drinks help in pushing my inhibitions aside as he takes off my shirt.

~ ~ ~

I wake up the next morning somewhat startled, wondering where I am. Then I remember. I'm at Max's house. I've spent many nights watching movies here. The innocence of us hanging out won't exactly be the same after last night. I find my glasses and put them on and begin searching for my clothes. There, by the door. I get dressed and leave before he wakes up.

I'm not entirely sure why I want to leave before I can speak to him. I know I'll text him later saying goodbye but first I need to think about what happened. I know I could have called Jenna and gotten a ride home but don't want to answer her questions yet, so I call a taxi.

I guess Max and I are together now. At least, I hope so.

I get home a little after 9 in the morning but I know he won't wake up on the weekend until noon at the earliest. I get home and get some instant oatmeal for breakfast because I can make it in my dorm room and read for a couple hours. When I know Max will start waking up soon, I text him:

Sorry I had to leave so early, I have some things to get done at home. Will I see you again before I leave? I'm free all weekend :)

I hit send and anxiously wait for a reply.

Chapter Two

There is nothing either good or bad, but thinking it makes it so - Hamlet, William Shakespeare

    He doesn't text me back before I leave. My Mom, Dad, little brother John and I arrive at the airport that Monday night.

    "Are you sure you have everything?" Mom asks. "Money? All your travel documents? Your passport?"

    "Mom, I'm not going to go to the airport without a passport. I double checked everything before we left."

I join the lineup to go through security and wave as my parents leave. I feel my eyes well up and I feel a hollow pain in my chest as I try to frantically open my carry-on suitcase and take out my laptop. The line is moving uncharacteristically fast and my vision is quickly blurring. Somehow I manage to get all my things in the appropriate bins and not beep as I go through the body scanner.

"You'll want this," the woman collecting the bins says as she tosses my phone to me. It's a miracle I caught it, given my history of being horrific at anything sports related. I have the worst hand-eye coordination in the world, the most athletic thing I can do is run at a snail's pace. I plug my headphones back in to my phone and turn on Reuben in the Dark, my current favourite band, though that changes frequently. My phone won't be that much use when I get to England but I can't fathom leaving it behind and not being able to have music during the summer.

I skipped breakfast and lunch today, so I decide I should probably eat something before I get on the flight and become trapped in a massive tin can hurtling me through the air. I look over the sandwich cart closest to my gate. It's late at night, so selection is slim. The only one that looks edible is a roast beef and cheddar with mayo oozing out of the sides of the bread. My stomach growls, reminding me how hungry I am. I turn over the plastic packaging and look at the nutrition label. 450 calories and 25 grams of fat. I buy it, a cheap coffee, and an apple and sit down by my gate. I throw away half of the sandwich and eat the rest.

There is next to nothing in the St. John's airport, and I am in serious need of a venti blonde roast. The cheap off-brand coffee will have to do instead.

I call Jenna to pass the time even though it's late.

"Hey," she says in a voice that is much too cheery for this hour at night. "I was hoping you would call. I'm sooooo bored and Steven already fell asleep."

"I have hours before I have to catch my flight so feel free to bug me."

"So are you going to tell me what happened at Max's?"

"Do I have to?"

"Yes, considering that I know it wasn't good. I was hoping it would be amazing but you've been in a bad mood since then so just tell me."

"Fine. I spent the night there. And we had sex. And that's it."

"That's it? Is he into anything weird? Wait, don't tell me, I don't want to know. So when are you guys making it official?"

"I don't know. We haven't spoken about it."

"Well you need to ask him."

"I will. Once I speak to him."

"So do it now."

"I've tried."

"You've… oh. Oh, I'm sorry."

"Me too."

"You know, this might not be all that bad. You don't want to be in a new relationship while you're gone. What if you meet someone new? That would be fun. Some hot British guy."

"Thanks but I'm not sure I want to. I'm just going to ignore him, unless he decides to text me back, until I get home. I don't want this trip to be spoiled with boy drama. I don't need Max or any other guy to have a good time."

"Yes. I love that. That's the way to think. Also shopping. Go shopping for something other than Converse and plain T-shirts and you will feel and look amazing."

"I will. I've already researched some running stores and they seem pretty good. A new workout outfit would be nice."

"I meant something fun and not an outfit used for torture, or as you call it, running, but that's a decent start I guess," she replies.

"Anyway, I guess I should go now. Thanks for letting me talk, I needed that."

"You know you can call me anytime, girl. Have a good flight. Also get me a shot glass while you're there."

"I will."

Not much is open with the exception of the one sandwich cart and a small gift shop. I buy a new book while I'm at the shop just in case I finish the one I brought. I sit at the gate with the sub par coffee from the sandwich cart and decide that will have to do and I wait until they call me for boarding.

When my gate is called, I board the plane and take my seat. The aircraft smells faintly of lemon scented cleaner and the stuffy air feels strangely comforting. I have a window seat, so it could be worse. I'm actually looking forward to the five hour flight. Being a student it's rare for me to have unlimited time to read and not feel like I should be doing homework. I'm rereading *Dracula* for this flight. A sweet looking older lady sits down in the seat next to me. I'm just hoping that she isn't someone who will want to talk the whole flight there. I never know how to brush people off when I don't want to talk to them. I probably just come off rude to most people but I think I'm just too introverted for my own good. I open my book as soon as she sits down, and leave in the earbud closest to the window and hope the flight attendant won't notice I'm listening to music during the safety instructions. Honestly, if this plane goes down I doubt we have much of a chance regardless of not paying attention to the safety instructions.

The elderly woman is wearing a mint green sweater that looks to be hand knit and matching mint green pants. She takes out a ball of yarn and a set of knitting needles as soon as we get in the air. I nickname her Bertha in my head because it sounds like an old lady name. She falls asleep holding her knitting as soon as the seatbelt sign goes off.

    Bertha wakes up as soon as the wheels of the plane hit the ground. I finished Dracula about an hour ago and I've been trying and failing to get some sleep for the rest of the flight. I'm excited and my heart begins to beat a little faster. I'm here. I'll completely forget about Max and just have fun and learn about theatre. Perfect. I pick up my bags pretty easily. Luckily nothing got lost, and I go to a kiosk to get my oyster card and a bus map. Now to find the Globe. I get a bus map from a stand in the train station - it doesn't look too difficult. Just… take a couple of bus transfers until I get there. I can manage this.

    I feel like a proper Londoner when I get off the bus close to the Waterloo station, until I realize I thought it was the closest station to the Globe. Apparently not, it's much closer to the London Eye and Big Ben, which I'm seeing for the first time since I got off the plane. The clock is smaller than I expected it to be but I have always admired its old world beauty. Especially in the same line of sight as the London Eye, which is the epitome of a modern landmark. It's amazing, but I can't stay. I have to check in to the campus. The day is a little overcast and gloomy but considering that I'm in London for the first time it's pretty close to perfect for me. I try not to look like a tourist but I think I'm failing considering that I'm holding a map of the South bank under my nose while trying to pull two suitcases. I'm almost dropping from exhaustion. I probably should have tried to sleep on the plane because I got no sleep last night. I didn't even want to look in the mirror when I went to the bathroom at the airport because I know it would be horrifying. I'm realizing it's not going to get any better when the torrential downpour begins.

Okay, maybe it's not that bad. But still. I haven't gotten an umbrella yet. I'm lost and soaked and tired. If this is a sign of how the rest of the summer is going to go then I'm pretty screwed. I know I should have seen this coming being that I'm in England. Except it's the middle of summer so I expected the weather to be a little better than the stereotype. After walking down the Thames for twenty minutes I'm soaked. My map is wet so I can't see where to go next and I have no idea how far away it is. My phone doesn't work for anything more than playing music while I'm here. Can you hail a cab in London like you see them do in movies set in New York? I have no idea. I don't know how to do that anyway.

Max would know what to do in a situation like this. He probably would have laughed it off and tell me something cliché like I needed to learn how to dance in the rain. He would have bought an umbrella and continued his way down to the Globe.

But I'm not Max. I'm Olivia. I'm an emotional wreck. So I decide to make the genius decision to sit on the sidewalk and have a good cry.

"Can I help you with something?" I hear a man ask. I look up and see a college age guy holding a blue umbrella. He sits down next to me so it's over both of us. "My name's Duncan." He holds out his hand. It's awkward because we're sitting next to each other instead of facing each other. It's also awkward because he's a beautiful dark haired and blued eyed man with a British accent and the rain makes my blonde hair plaster on to my fair skin so look like a drowned albino rat.

"Olivia." I shake his hand.

"It's nice to meet you Olivia. Are you American?"

"Canadian," I'd been warned about this before I left. I forgot to get a Canadian flag to put on my jacket so people would know where I'm from.

"So what are you doing out here in the rain all by yourself? Aren't you traveling with anyone?" He asks me. Now that I think about it there's really no one else out here. I'm all alone with no phone to call for help and no one expecting me back home anytime soon. I start to panic. I'm going to be kidnapped on my first day here. I stand up.

"Um, no, I'm not here alone. My boyfriend came with me and I need to leave now to meet him." For someone who studies theatre arts, this is a terrible performance.

"You don't know me, I get that. At least tell me where you're going so you don't get lost again."

"Okay, fine. I'm going to the Globe Theatre. I don't need you to walk me there, just point me in the right direction."

"The Globe? Yeah, it's that way. You're about a twenty-five minute walk away," he chuckles. "Hope you get there okay. Never know, I might see you around." He walks in the opposite direction of where I'm supposed to go.

Finally, I reach The Globe. It looks exactly like it does in the pictures I saw online. It's a small building but it looks like it's towering over the ones surrounding it. A large schedule stats what's playing this season. *Macbeth, A Midsummer Night's Dream*, and *Love's Labour's Lost* are among them. Three of my favourites. Yes, I followed Duncan's directions. Not because I trust him but because I was really lost. I arrive in just about the same amount of time as he said I would. Maybe he is trustworthy, but I wasn't about to take my chances. According to the program guide I got in the mail a few weeks ago I'm supposed to check in at the front desk of the museum and someone will help me from there.

"Hi. You must be here for the college program?" A perky woman whose name tag claims she is Mary Beth, greets me. "Someone will be here any minute to walk you to your room in The Commons. It's really close by, just down the road, but we still like to give you a warm welcome here so you're not walking there alone! Here's the room key. Your roommate already checked in," just as she finishes, another woman, Leanne, walks in. The rain has stopped by now but I can see Leanne has an umbrella clipped to her belt. Smart girl.

We reach the campus and I use a small white card Leanne gave to me to open the sliding glass doors of the old looking brick building. I see signs pointing in directions of dorm rooms, offices, and classrooms, and can still see The Globe in the distance. My room key had 457 printed on the back so I drag my heavy suitcases up the stairs up to the fourth floor. I feel light headed when I finally reach the top, and wonder if someone has told the British that elevators were invented for situations like this. When I open the door to my room it's obvious my roommate has already settled in. There are pictures of people who I assume are her friends on one side of the room. I hear someone come out of the bathroom.

"Hey, I'm Tiana," she waves at me. She seems nice enough.

"I'm Olivia."

"So, Olivia. Tell me about yourself. Where are you from? What's your major?" She asks as she sits on her bed.

"I'm Canadian. English and Theatre Arts double major."

"Cool. I'm American, from Virginia Beach. I'm a fashion design major with a concentration in historical fashions. I'm assuming you want to perform at the end of the summer? I'm mostly here for the costume design aspect."

Tiana's a beautiful woman. She has long dark hair styled in braided curls. A couple of the braids are red, and some blonde, but most of them are a rich brown. Her black skin has a dewy glow. I make a mental note to ask about her skin care routine, maybe she could help with my acne problems.

"Yeah, I mean I'm hoping I at least get a speaking role. But it's my first year so I'll probably be an extra."

"I should say something more encouraging but that's true. Some of these people are in their fourth year and have been coming since they were freshmen. Some even have family members who work here so they know everyone involved in the productions. It's my second summer here so I know how competitive they can be. I need to call home. You don't mind if I make a call do you?"

"Go ahead, I need to get ready and go to bed. I'm really tired."

I try and fail to take a nap. Normally naps come second - or, let's be honest, first - nature to me but my mind is racing. It's hard to believe I'm in London. I'm outside of Canada for the first time ever and here I am, at a campus with a stranger after narrowly escaping certain demise at the hand of a beautiful British stranger. He's cute though. I briefly regret not getting his number, but better safe than sorry.

I finally doze off for a minute, and before I know it I'm dreaming.

I'm in the woods on my back and there is a horrible stranger, some man much bigger than me, sitting on my chest. I'm blinded except for seeing his laughing smile. I smell the dirt and sweat radiating off his body. I try to push him off of me but he's too strong for me and I lay glued to the ground. My fingernails dig in to the earth and all I can do is grasp the filth. His hand starts slowly touching my thigh, and I gasp myself awake.

"Are you okay, or are you like epileptic or something?" Tiana asks when I wake up.

"No. Just a bad dream."

"Are you one of those people who wakes up with night terrors every night? Am I going to get PTSD because I'm your roommate? Because if you are I'm going to go to housing right now. I'm *so* not rooming with a freak."

"I'm *not* a freak." I say defiantly and get out of bed. I need to go for a walk.

"Well… okay, that was rude. Sorry. I just had a really bad experience with my roommate last year and I don't want to go through all that again."

"It's fine. I'm going for a walk."

"Sure. Dinner is at 6, so if you want to go with me and sit with my friends you can."

I have two hours and I plan to be out for as much of it as possible.

I don't go too far, but I do decide to walk around the Thames. The sun is peeking out of the clouds and reflecting off the pavement, making the day look nicer than it really is. The sun is gently setting over the river. There's a Starbucks close by, so I head in and get my long awaited coffee. I take it back out to the river and jump up on one of the stone bricks and sit there with my legs crossed and just watch everyone walk by. There's rich looking people walking little white dogs, running groups racing past me, and babies screaming in their strollers. I wonder how many of them are regulars here and how many are here for the first time, like myself.

There's a boy with a huge backpack that must weigh as much as he does with a map stuck under his nose. He must be a tourist, too. I feel bad for him and wish I could help him find his way but I would be as lost as he is. I wonder if I'll ever feel comfortable getting around in a city bigger than St. John's.

I see Tiana walk by laughing with a small slender girl with long, auburn hair. Tiana links her arm in with the girl's and they glide past the Starbucks, not looking my way. I become intensely aware that I'm here by myself and begin to wonder if coming here was such a good idea after all.

Chapter Three

By the pricking of my thumbs, something wicked this way comes - Macbeth, William Shakespeare

    "Are you coming to dinner?" Tiana tentatively asks me, "I'm sorry about what I said earlier today. If it helps, you can meet my friends while we're there. They're great, you'll love them."

    "Yeah, just give me a sec. Is there a scale in any of the rooms?" I ask.

"No, they don't have any. Huh, I probably should get one. I can't be bothered most mornings though. There's a gym on the third floor, I think they might have one. It'll be one of those big scales they have at the doctor's."

"I'm going to run down real quick. Just give me a minute." I brush my teeth and hair and put on a pair of sweatpants and clean shirt. At least now I don't feel like a total zombie.

I take the stairs down to the third floor and step on the scale. It's a little higher than I expected, so I'll have to go low carb for as long as possible. I'm mostly afraid this will be like most study abroad trips my friends have told me about and ends up with everyone drinking at least 600 calories of alcohol every night. I take a quick look around the gym to see what they have: an old treadmill, some weights that are mostly all there, and a couple of balance balls. I'll have to just run outside while I'm here.

I meet up with Tiana and we take the stairs down one level to the main floor where they have a buffet style dinner set up. The salad bar seems pretty fresh so I fill my dinner plate with that. I pick up one of the small bowls and mix two tablespoons of olive oil with four tablespoons of balsamic vinegar, and just a few croutons, and a mini quiche and follow Tiana to the table with her friends.

"Hello, Olivia," a vaguely familiar voice says.

"Hey... Duncan, right?" I look up and am surprised as to who I see. Well, apparently I could have trusted the guy.

"You two know each other?" Tiana asks.

"We met yesterday. He gave me directions on how to get here. Speaking of yesterday, why didn't you come straight here?"

"Well I thought you might think I was stalking you. But no really, a friend was dropping me off after I finished up a walk. I was going back to his flat."

I realize everyone else at the table is staring at us.

"Apparently you already know Duncan. This is Harper," the short girl with auburn hair that I saw with Tiana earlier looks up at me. She has a book in her lap. I think I will get along with her just fine. "And my boyfriend, James," he's sitting across from me. He's tall with blonde hair and blue eyes. "Harper and Duncan are both from England and James and I grew up together. Guys, this is my roommate, Olivia."

"Hopefully she's better than your roommate last year" Harper says in a hushed tone. Everyone else laughs.

"I'll explain later," Tiana says to me.

"Hey guys, if I could just get your attention," someone says at the front of the room. "I'm Marcus and I'm going to be your coordinator for your time here. I'll be the one addressing you with all the important info, like role placements. I just wanted to say hi and introduce myself so you all know who I am. My room is 107 just in case you need anything. I'll be staying here in the campus with you. Classes begin Monday at 9 A.M. You should have found a class schedule in your rooms. Attendance is mandatory. I hope you're all prepared." With that he leaves, and my time in England officially begins.

"What are you doing after dinner?" James asks Tiana.

"Not sure yet, but you know me. Love fresh meat on move in day so I'll probably take Olivia to lose her London virginity."

"I'm not really sure I'm up for too much today. I'm not still tired but I'm still jet lagged."

"We won't go too far in to London, just around campus - the area around the Globe and The Commons, it's not a big area. You'll want to know where everything is, right? Look, you'll love it. And if you're too tired you can be home in like five minutes, tops."

"Tiana, don't coerce her in to hanging out with you," James says.

"No, it's fine. I came here to explore so might as well do it," I say and take another bite of dinner.

"Okay, good. I've been planning it ever since I found out I was getting a random for a roommate. Not to call you a random, I mean you're great but we just met. Anyway, we need to go to the Rose Theatre today and see the excavation site. We'll need to walk the Thames with a can of Strongbow and make fun of tourists," Tiana says.

"Hey," I say in mock offence.

"You're not a tourist anymore, Olivia. I'll get you all trained until you're one of the locals. Don't worry. You almost done?" Tiana asks, impatiently waiting for me to finish so we can leave. Everyone else has finished eating, so I awkwardly eat the last bites of salad and gulp down the rest of my coffee.

"I need a shower before we leave," I say as we wave at everyone and leave to go back upstairs.

"Yes, you do. You smell like an airport," Tiana says.

I shower first, because I have to dry my hair when I get out of the shower. I take my clothes off and drop them on the clean tile I turn the water on far too hot and step inside. I flinch as the hot water hits my skin but feel immediate relief. The last time I took a shower was the day after I slept with Max. It feels like a lifetime away already. I feel a hole in my chest when I think of how much I miss him and how much I wish he would text me back. I want to let him know I landed. I want him to care.

"You take forever in the shower," Tiana says when I get out.

"Sorry. Long couple of days. It won't be that bad next time."

"What's wrong?" She asks.

"I'll talk about it when we're walking."

About an hour later when we leave the room, I'm thankful for the fresh air. I can smell the Thames river and the overcast day is damp and refreshing.

"So which guy stepped on your heart?" Tiana asks.

"How did you know?"

"I've been around, I know when a guy has been a little bit of a shit."

"There is someone at home."

"And?"

"And we slept together, and he won't text me back. He might just be busy though."

"He's probably not busy. I hate boys."

"This is the Rose," Tiana says when we approach an industrial looking building. We had to wind down a couple of narrow streets to get here. We aren't the only people on the street but it's much quieter compared to how busy the Thames is. Tiana knocks on the heavy door and it swings open.

"Tiana," The woman inside says and smiles at us, "come in, I'm just eating my dinner." I see an open tupperware container with a slice of pizza inside, "I'm so glad you're back. Who's with you?"

"This is Olivia, my roomie for the summer. Olivia, this is Jane. She's an old vet of the program."

"I came for the summer after graduation and never left. Managed to get a full time job here as soon as it finished, and now I'm leading tour groups. Have you been to London before?"

I shake my head.

"You'll love it. Well, this is the Rose," she says and waves her arms to the room she lets us in to. There are red lines that illuminate the floor in the shape of a small area.

"What is it?" I ask.

"It's a theatre. There were lots in this area," Jane says.

"Why?"

"Because the South bank used to be pretty trashy. There was drinking and prostitution in the streets, and theatre wasn't a respected art. They essentially stuck all the theatres down here and let everyone travel to the South bank for their entertainment. The Rose was a theatre like the Globe. The Swan was also pretty close by. They found this site a couple of years ago. Actors and directors from all over the city protested to keep the Rose here instead of destroying what was left of it," Jane says.

"That's so cool," I say.

"It really is amazing. That's where the stage was, and that's the seating area. It was a small theatre. I do tours of the neighbourhood now, too. I show people around here and where the Globe originally was."

I knew already that the Globe standing today is a recreation. The second, actually. I guess that's what happens when someone builds a building made of flammable materials and no sprinkler system.

"Show Olivia your ring, Jane," Tiana says.

"It's a replica of one they found here at the excavation site." She puts her hand out in front of me. A small silver band wraps around her middle finger and has an inscription I can't read on it.

"What does it say?"

"*Pences pov r moy e dv*," Jane says.

I give her a confused look in return.

"It means "think of my, God willing" in Latin."

"That's so cool," I eye the ring longingly.

"You can buy it at the Globe gift shop. Yes, I wear something I got from the gift shop from my place of work, to my place of work. I'm a nerd."

"I think you two will get along just fine," Tiana says and laughs at us.

We hang out with Jane for another forty five minutes until her lunch break is over and she has to give another tour.

"Now what?" I ask Tiana.

"Drinks, I think."

"You know it's our first day here and we can't be hungover for classes, right?"

"You're on vacation. You're allowed to live a little. Besides, you'll be swamped with work before you know it. I need to make you have as much fun as possible while we still can."

We approach the door to a building that looks like it should be someone's home, but the small sign above the door claims it's "The Crown: Traditional English Pub".

We walk in and hear music flowing through the speakers at a lower level than I am used to, but it's nice to be able to hear myself think in a bar - or excuse me, pub.

"Glad to see you girls finally made it," James says as we approach the table he sits at.

"Where's Harper?" I ask, looking around. It's just Duncan and James with us in the pub.

"She won't be here today. Her parents are in town for their last night for a while, so she's spending some time with them." Duncan pushes his dark framed glasses further up on his nose and shoots at dart at the board on the wall. It bounces off the side of the board and sticks in to wooden floor.

"I think you've had one too many drinks tonight, Dun," James says and picks up the dart and puts it in the holder by the board.

Duncan orders us a round of cider and we sit at the booth in the corner of the room. James puts his arms around Tiana and she snuggles into him.

"Think we should let them be alone for, oh I don't, know, about three minutes?" Duncan says and punches James in the shoulder.

"Ow," James says, rubbing the spot Duncan hit. "Asshole. And it does not take three minutes, thank you."

"Sure it doesn't."

"So tell us about yourself, Olivia. What's your story?" Duncan says.

"Pretty run of the mill. Canadian. Student. English and Theatre. Had to get away from home so I ran to the country of tea and biscuits."

"Tea and biscuits we do have. I'm glad you're here. What classes are you taking?"

"Shakespearean Comedies, Shakespearean Tragedies, Intro to Costume Design, and Intro to Performing."

"Cool, we'll have Comedies together," he says excitedly.

"Are there any professors I should watch out for? I need to get good grades this summer. All my classes are transferrable."

"Yeah, Banner is pretty tough, but he wants your performance to get better. I don't like Mr. Barnes much either. He's kind of creepy. Like, I wouldn't want any of my friends to run into him alone at night. I'm sure you'll be fine though."

"Hopefully," I say, "so what's *your* story?"

"Wouldn't you like to know," he says and winks at me.

My heart flutters in my chest just a moment before Max's face flashes in my head. Duncan is nice but I have someone else at home. I'm sure Max will text me back when he can. I take out my phone and connect to The Crown's wifi.

Should I text Max? I ask Jenna through my messenger app.

No, you already did it once. That's enough. She says in response.

"Lets play a game of darts and leave the love birds to themselves," Duncan says and nods toward Tiana and James.

"I don't know, I'm pretty buzzed. I might not be that good."

"Perfect. That just means I'll seem like a better player than I am." He holds his hand out to me to help me out of the booth.

I throw my first dart and land on a twenty.

"So is that good or bad?" I ask.

"Pretty good, actually," he says and takes his shot. A five.

"Ha! I guess I'm better at this than I thought."

"You must be. So, Olivia, do you have a boyfriend back in Canada?"

"Wouldn't you like to know." I smirk at him and take my next shot.

We continue playing until it comes down to the both of us with five points left.

"There's no way you're just as good as I am," I say, "you're letting me win."

"No I'm not," he says. He seems slightly frightened and I actually believe he's not letting me win.

I take my last shot and land right in the middle of the five. I yell out and throw my hands up in the air and I see a look of despair wash over Duncan's face.

"Hey, Duncan," Fleur says from the doorway of the room we're in.

"Hey, Fleur."

"Who's your friend?"

"This is Olivia. You're not allowed to talk to her or you'll corrupt her."

"Dun," she pouts, "you love me, though, remember?" She walks up to him and slips her arm around his waist.

"That, I do not," Duncan says. She seems slightly crazy to me, but by looking at her I have to assume Duncan likes her more than he leads on.

"*Je peux vous offrir un verre?*" Fleur flirts with Duncan.

"*Non, je voudrais que tu partes*," he replies.

She sees someone on the other side of the pub waving at her and winks at Duncan once before heading off in his direction.

"What was all that?" I ask.

"She wanted to buy me a drink. I told her to sod off."

I stare at him blankly.

"Fuck off. I told her to fuck off. You need to get used to the English way of speaking, mate."

"I don't want to mate with you."

He rolls his eyes at me. "Sure you don't."

"I don't!"

"No, but I do," James says behind us and smacks Duncan on the ass.

"I would have but you never let me," Duncan says.

"Maybe I changed my mind."

"That's your boyfriend," Duncan says to Tiana, pointing at James. "There is no way you find this acceptable."

"Acceptable? I think this is great. Super hot. Next, you need to fight over me."

I laugh at Tiana and James. Their relationship seems so fun and effortless, and I wonder if I'll ever have anything like that. I know I'm only twenty and there's more than enough time to find someone I click with who will sleep with me and still call me back the next day, but I can't help but hope for it. I've been afraid to be in a relationship with some since… well, since forever. Since I was a kid. Since Michael.

"What's wrong?" Duncan asks.

"Nothing." I take a drink and try to smile, "I'm fine."

Chapter Four

Stars, hide your fires; Let not light see my black and deep desires - Macbeth, William Shakespeare

I hear a quick knock and Tiana enters the room.

"Look what I have," she grins as she holds up two tickets. "Apparently the Globe has a box reserved just for employees and their friends. We are now friends, and soon to be employees so we get free tickets. Duncan and James already have theirs. It starts in an hour, I'm getting ready now." She drops the tickets on her nightstand and goes to the bathroom to take a shower. I glance down at the tickets on the table. They're for today's showing of Macbeth. It's one of the plays I especially want to see during my stay, so I also decide to get ready. I should go out and do something fun instead of brood about Max. It's day three here and he already hasn't texted me back. I decide to go against my own rule and text him once more saying "hi", but I almost don't expect a response any more.

    I hear my computer beep and go over to check who it is. It's a message from Max.

Hey, sorry I couldn't respond earlier. I was busy. Hope you're having fun in London and I'll probably see you when you get back.

    It's not exactly the romantic response I was hoping for. I was secretly wishing he would be anxiously waiting the three days to respond to me. I think that rule is pointless but I still hope that's why he wasn't talking to me. I decide to ignore it for now and knew I needed to talk to Jenna before I said anything back to him. If he shrugs me off there's no reason why I should have to talk to him right away anyway.

    I struggle for a minute to pick what to wear - Jenna always overpacks, but I guess I can't complain if I didn't do it myself. I pick a simple pair of blue jeans and a white chiffon top, and a white flower clip to keep my side swept bangs out of my face. I haven't seen the inside of the theatre yet, but I hope it looks like the picture I've seen online. With getting settled away and getting ready for classes I'm busier than I expected. I'm so ready to finally see it. When Tiana finishes getting ready – I'm beginning to notice it takes her a good thirty minutes longer than it takes me – the boys show up to walk us over.

"Ladies," James playfully bows and links arms with Tiana.

"Better stop being so cute or Olivia will end up stealing you away from me," Tiana said and kisses James on the cheek. Duncan rolls his eyes at me.

I have to keep my jaw from dropping when I walk in to the theatre. It's just as beautiful as in the photos I've studied for years. The open ceiling is perfect for summer nights like this one. We're some of the first ones here so we get to sit in the box for a while with the almost empty theatre and just take in the architecture. The ceilings above us and above the stage are decorated to look like the night sky and with figures of the zodiac. The stage is set differently than the photos I've seen. The red marble columns are covered with a spooky black and white decoration to make them suit the mood of Macbeth better. The four of us talk for a bit while we're waiting for the play to start but I'm not paying much attention. I'm mainly trying to take it all in.

The show starts with a bang. Loud, dramatic music, exactly the right thing to set the mood for such a play. The man playing Macbeth has a huge stage presence. He's a short man with a thick black beard, and was so in character that during some of the shouting lines he nearly spits on some of the people in the front of the standing area. The acting is incredible and I can tell the whole crowd is enthralled with the performance. The final scene ends and it takes a moment for any of us to say anything.

"That was amazing," Tiana finally breaks the silence.

"Incredible," James agrees.

"I'm exhausted, you know it's past my bedtime. You guys ready to walk home?" Tiana asks.

"Actually, I wanted to go for a cup of tea. Are you coming, Olivia?" Duncan says.

"Yeah for sure."

We walk with James and Tiana back to The Comms and I turn to walk in the small cafe next to the lobby of the campus.

"Actually, there's somewhere else I want to take you. It's not far away," he says.

We can't stop talking about the performance on our way there.

"I'm a big fan of Macbeth. My parents met in Scotland at production of it. She was a stage hand and he knew the person playing Duncan. Dad's friend let him come backstage and meet everyone. Apparently Dad didn't know much about theatre and the culture around it. He was saying 'Macbeth' all around the theatre. A lot of people there didn't believe in the curse but Mum did. She marched right up to him and told him off about what he was saying. He told me he was a little taken aback by this woman shouting at him but he noticed how passionately she cared for her work. He said he insisted on her coming back to the pub with him and teaching him all about the theatre. So she did. I don't even think she really liked him to begin with. She just wanted to teach someone else about proper stage etiquette. Anyway, they stayed in that pub all night just talking. They spent the next week together until Dad had to go home to England and Mom got a placement at the Piccadilly Theatre here in London. You might have heard of it," he winks at me. "They moved in together almost right away and have been together ever since. They decided to name me after that play because it's what brought them together."

"That's great. It's much more romantic than a real love story that I've ever heard." Wow, Olivia. He spills out his life story and that's all you have to say? *Wonderful.*

He opens the door of the café for me and a little bell on the door frame rings. It's a small hole in the wall place with a small sign above the door saying 'The Muse' and the one window on the door was almost completely covered by an "open 24/7" sign.

This place is glorious.

There are books stacked floor-to-ceiling and a single barista sits at the counter reading a book and sipping out of a tiny espresso cup. All the decor is red, black, and gold, like a vintage theatre. There are a few patrons, most of which reading and sipping on coffee but one was writing in a notebook. I wonder what exactly he's writing. As someone who frequents this place, it's probably the next *Moby Dick* or *Pride and Prejudice*. I can see why this is a place that appeals to writers. With being open all hours of the day and night it will service night owls and morning people alike. I was much more of a night owl so I knew I would be by here more often when I can't sleep. Granted, the caffeine won't help so I hope they have a selection of herbal teas I could have at night.

Duncan and I sit down at a spot away from the barista.

"What do you want?" Duncan asks.

"Whatever your favourite is," I reply.

He smiles at me and goes over to the counter.

I get up and look around at some of the titles. Many are old and rare books. Probably not first editions or they would be under lock and key but they're still much nicer and more interesting than anything else I've seen before. I pick a few up off the shelf and begin flipping through them. Gorgeous editions, good condition, and fairly priced. I know I'll be coming back.

Duncan returns, somehow managing to balance two plates, and two mugs each, with a piece of cheesecake and a steaming green tea.

"Careful or you'll spill it all over yourself," I say and quickly take a mug and plate.

"I brought a cheesecake with a strawberry topping – the best you'll ever have, and a green tea. Not too much caffeine, as you'll probably want to sleep sometime tonight, but I don't want you falling asleep on me. I hope you like green tea, I forgot to ask but I'm pretty good at guessing which tea someone will like," he says.

"You're in luck since I'll drink just about anything. English breakfast is my favourite though," I say.

"Good choice. I'll remember it for next time. So I see you've found something of interest?" he asks, nodding to the books I replaced when he was getting back.

"Yeah, these are really beautiful. I took a class on print history last year and it really got me into things that were from the earliest printing periods. People have no idea where something that surrounds us came from."

"That's really interesting. I've collected some of the books I found here over time. I would like to get more but I'm running out of shelf space. I think it's high time I got another bookshelf." Over our desert and tea we talk about some of our favourite books and then we browse the selection for a while. I end up leaving with a copy of *Ovid* and *Beowulf*, Duncan leaving with *Aesop's Fables*.

I wonder why he brought me here. Certainly he can't he interested in me, right? I've put on thirty pounds since last summer. Sure, that was when I was in recovery at the eating disorder clinic, but still. I can still see myself get puffy and bloated when I've eaten too much that day. I still think I was fat when I was admitted in to recovery. There is no way Duncan will go for me when Fleur is trying to hook up with him.

"So have you ever dated Fleur?" I ask.

"What makes you ask that?"

"Oh, it just seemed like it, you know? From the way she was hanging off you yesterday."

"Yes, Mum. I'll be good," he chuckles, "enough about her for now. Are you ready to leave?" He takes the last bite of his cheesecake and brings our dishes up to the counter.

It's a nice night. It's slightly warmer than it was yesterday, and the stars are out tonight, and I gaze up at them as we walk back to the campus.

"You like the stars?" Duncan asks.

"Yeah, I do. I'm not very good at astronomy, though."

"Here. Lay down with me." Duncan gets on his back on the rough cobblestone road.

"You can't be serious. There must be dirt on that road from a horse's hoof from like the fourteenth century," I cross my arms in front of my chest and look down at him.

"I'm dead serious. I'm black plague infested dirt serious. Here, lay down." He pats the ground beside him. I reluctantly lay down next to him and hope there's nothing crawling on the ground that will soon be crawling on me.

"See that star over there?" He asks and points to the sky.

"Yes."

"That one is Pegasus."

"The unicorn?"

"Pegasus is not a unicorn. He's a flying horse. Big difference."

"Ah, I see. Well, I don't see. I should say I understand. I don't see anything besides a bunch of stars."

"You should. He was created by Poseidon, the god of the sea. Poseidon used Pegasus to defeat Medusa, the Gorgon."

"Who?"

"How do you not know who Medusa is? You're a Shakespeare buff, you should know all this stuff."

"Which one was Medusa in *Romeo and Juliet*? She was a Montague, right? Duncan, I hardly know who I am half the time."

"Well, she was evil. Like, really bad. She had snakes for hair and if you looked in to her eyes she would turn you to stone."

"She must have been fun on dates."

"She wasn't, which is probably why Poseidon dumped her. Any way, she got really mad and kind of went crazy."

"Hopefully Fleur was nicer to you when you guys broke up."

"I didn't say we broke up."

"You implied it."

"I know some of the stories, sure. I know Cupid and Psyche, of course, from *A Midsummer Night's Dream,* and Hercules from *The Merchant of Venice*... that kind of stuff. I've studied the mythology in plays, but it's a lot to keep track of and I get the names mixed up. And I've never really looked at the constellations.

"Well I think you should look at the stars more."

"Maybe," I say, my eyelids getting heavy.

"You look tired," Duncan says and yawns. Before getting up. He reaches his hand out to help me up off the ground and we both wipe the dust off our clothes and start walking home.

"Don't forget the books you bought," he says and points and them on the ground.

"So you know we can't keep hanging out if you are going to encourage me to keep buying books," I say as we approach the front door of The Commons.

"Well, you know, I'm just such a bad influence," he says.

Duncan slips his hands in to his jeans pockets. He looks like he's going to lean in to kiss me, but instead he chuckles and says, "well it's getting late. I guess I'll see you around." He gives me a small wave and quickly turns on his heel and goes up the stairs, toward his room.

Chapter Five

Cry havoc and let slip the dogs of war! - Julius Caesar, William Shakespeare

I wake up to Tiana's face in my face.

"You planning on waking up today?" She asks.

"Not if I can help it." I pull the blanket over my head and roll over.

"I'm on my way down to breakfast. Classes start in half an hour." She crosses her arms and looks down at me.

Shit. Shit shit shit shit. I'm going to be late for class.

I jump up and run in to the bathroom, brushing my hair and teeth at the same time. I put on a pair of black yoga pants, a plain green t-shirt and a brown sweatshirt with the Memorial University logo on it. It's not exactly what I would have picked out if I had time but it will have to do. I know it'll take about ten minutes to get to class and I've spent five minutes getting ready already. I dart down to the breakfast bar and quickly eat a slice of toast and gulp down some orange juice and take an apple for my walk there.

I manage to make it to the Globe just in time for class to start. Most classes are in The Commons, but because this is a performance class, we get to use The Globe's stage. The professor is at the front of the room and I notice Harper is sitting in the middle-front row of the stands. I sit down next to her just as he begins speaking.

"My name is Mr. Barnes and I will be teaching you stage performance this term, I'll also be directing the final performance you'll be working toward all term. I know you are all here to land a lead role. If you're not, then please leave," everyone sits in silence. "Good. Now, Shakespeare was the greatest playwright to ever touch pen to paper. I trust you will all do him, and this temple we work in, justice." This guy is intense. I love Shakespeare and all but I don't know if I would call him the greatest to ever write. I, however, am going to leave that opinion to myself.

"You'll find the first text we'll be studying on your desk. This will not necessarily be the text we perform though. This is just a warm up," I pick up the copy of *Hamlet* he provided us with. This is going to be relatively easy. I'd played Ophelia in my high school's production of *Hamlet*.

"Who would like to begin with a recitation of Hamlet's to be or not to be speech? I trust you all have it memorized, this is a pretty fundamental text." Uh, oh. I don't know it *that* well.

"I'll do it," I hear a someone with a French accent say from the back of the room.

"Wonderful, Fleur," the professor says.

She stands up, clears her throat, and begins, "To be, or not to be--that is the question:

Whether 'tis nobler in the mind to suffer
The slings and arrows of outrageous fortune
Or to take arms against a sea of troubles
And by opposing end them. To die, to sleep--
No more--and by a sleep to say we end
The heartache, and the thousand natural shocks
That flesh is heir to. 'Tis a consummation
Devoutly to be wished. To die, to sleep--
To sleep--perchance to dream: ay, there's the rub,
For in that sleep of death what dreams may come
When we have shuffled off this mortal coil,

Must give us pause. There's the respect
That makes calamity of so long life.
For who would bear the whips and scorns of time,
Th' oppressor's wrong, the proud man's contumely
The pangs of despised love, the law's delay,
The insolence of office, and the spurns
That patient merit of th' unworthy takes,
When he himself might his quietus make
With a bare bodkin? Who would fardels bear,
To grunt and sweat under a weary life,
But that the dread of something after death,
The undiscovered country, from whose bourn
No traveller returns, puzzles the will,
And makes us rather bear those ills we have
Than fly to others that we know not of?
Thus conscience does make cowards of us all,
And thus the native hue of resolution
Is sicklied o'er with the pale cast of thought,
And enterprise of great pitch and moment
With this regard their currents turn awry
And lose the name of action. -- Soft you now,
The fair Ophelia! -- Nymph, in thy orisons
Be all my sins remembered."

    "Ah, lovely, Fleur, simply lovely," Mr. Barnes claps. During the speech she manages to mask her obvious French heritage and put on a seamless English accent.
    "See, ladies and gentlemen, this is my best student. She's been under my wing for years. She landed the role of Juliet in her first summer here. This is what you should aim to be," he motions to her and she takes a small curtsey before sitting back down.

"Oh, Mr. Barnes, you are simply too kind," she flashes a set of perfectly white and straight teeth.

For the rest of the class he gave each of us a monologue to perform. Luckily he let us use the scripts he gives us.

Costume design is interesting, even though I know I'll never have the passion for it Tiana does. She's in the more advanced class than I am so we don't have that one together either. My professor has a grand air about her and is dressed in what I would consider a costume, a big pink ball gown with big rhinestones on the bodice and obviously dyed platinum hair. Harper assures me that's her daily uniform and she is, indeed, as crazy as she looks.

"What do you have next?" Harper asks me when we're leaving the classroom.

"Intro to set design."

"Great, I'm in that too."

"Why are you in an intro class?"

"There isn't a huge selection in classes, so I'm retaking this one. My university will let me get credit for it twice, so might as well. The classes are all really different from year to year, and the prof for that class loves me, so might as well go and help her out."

"What's the class like?"

"Starts with history of stage performance. You know, how they used to do special effects."

"You mean how they used to use a cannon to make the thundering noises in *Macbeth*?"

"Exactly like that. We don't get to demonstrate that, I'm afraid. Any way, back stage is as choreographed as what's on stage. It's a seriously under appreciated art."
"I can imagine."
"You don't have to. You're going to learn it in class."
"Yeah… I know. It's just a phrase."
"Oh."

We spend this class behind the scenes watching one of the Performances at the Globe. The older students like Harper do their usual part to help the performers, the rest of us stand in a designated safe area where we're out of the way.

Harper was right when she said it was a well choreographed performance. I can hear the professional actors performing their lines from *King Lear*, and I know what is happening based on which actors are backstage, either waiting for their next turn or quickly changing costumes.

Some of the actors are still putting on the final touches of their makeup. The pop up changing stalls are being set up for when the actors need to change and want privacy. Some people have as little as a minute to put on three layers of clothing that have to be placed just perfectly and not disturb their makeup or wig, if they're wearing one.

Harper is directing the performers to the best places for them to stand while they're waiting for their cue. Most of them know this any way because it's practiced so much, but Harper acts like a ringleader in the circus. Everyone knows their cue but we're all human, except for Harper. She seems to keep the whole show together.

"That was awesome," I say when the show is over and all the actors are taking their bow, and Harper's job is finally done.

"I always love show days. I was a bit rusty since it's been so long since I've been here. My school doesn't have the best theatre program. I volunteer backstage in the community when I can but still I get out of practice during the school year."

"Why did you pick your university if it doesn't have a good theatre program? That is your major, right?"

"Yeah but it's cheap. Mom and Dad started the divorce process when I was a senior in high school. They kind of dragged me in to it. Any way, it's expensive. Lawyers and stuff."

"That's fucked up. I'm sorry."

"Yeah, it is what it is. At least my Grandma can pay for my summers here. Cheaper than a good school."

"That's nice of her."

I return to my room before dinner and Tiana is already there.

"So I have a couple of classes with Harper," I say.

"Yeah? That's awesome."

"Also Fleur, the one I saw at the Crown hitting on Duncan the other night."

"No way, really? Harper should have immediately texted me when she knew she was in that class. And yeah, she's super trashy. She thinks all the guys want to hook up with her, even when they don't." Tiana lifts the lid to her laptop and begins typing at who I assume is Harper. "So what happened?"

"She is a total teacher's pet. She started reciting a monologue from Hamlet upon request. I thought I knew the play, I mean I even performed in it, but damn I could never do that," I say.

"Yeah don't worry too much about her. She always gets the lead. Her Dad's super rich and I think he knows some people who work here. Probably the program director or a couple of the profs." Her laptop beeps and she types something back. "So tell me all about it. Were her clones there?"

"Half the girls at this school are just alike. You'll have to be more specific."

"Rosie, Mary, and Cathy. They're the ones who follow her around all the time. They all have long blonde hair - I mean, no offence. You're nothing like them - " I run my hair through the bottom of my shoulder length blonde hair, "and blue eyes. They always wear those awful Ugg boots." Tiana fake shudders.

"Oh yeah they were with her. I'm starting to think they always are. What exactly happened with you two?"

"She was my roommate first year. We were actually really good friends. Fleur is from Paris but she went to the same University as me in Virginia Beach. She's studying English and Performing Arts like you are. Going to an English speaking country was one of the requirements for her degree. She has some family in Virginia so that's where she chose. Anyway, we became good friends. She told me about this program and we both applied, and both got in. We thought it would be the perfect summer. I mean, London in the summer with one of your best friends should be perfect, right? But no, the competition got the best of us and we stopped talking."

"Why would you two be competing? You aren't in the same major. You don't even want to perform."

"That's not the only way people compete. Besides, we lived right next to Harper so I got close with her as well and she wanted to perform. She only really wanted a small role because her heart is still in the backstage work. But you know how auditions are. You audition for everything and they put you where you best fit. Harper is a better actress than she seems, and she's really great at memorizing lines. She's got a good rapport with the profs that do the casting. It was too much for Fleur and she felt threatened. I would help Harper practice and modify her costume to make it look amazing on her. And I am very skilled, mind you. Fleur didn't like all the attention I was paying to Harper. She didn't think she deserved it."

"That really sucks. I mean I know why she would want your fabulous design skills, and you better not neglect me to help Harper out more," I smile at her.

"Never, Sweetie. *Tu mon cherie.* Like clay I will mould you into a star," she says in an exaggerated French accent. I laugh and hit her with my pillow.

Chapter Six

For she had eyes and chose me - Othello, William Shakespeare

    I hear a knock on my door. Today is one of our "cultural days". When I asked Tiana what that was, she said it was just a day off. We're encouraged to go out to a museum or something to take it British culture. Most people spent it at the local pubs trying to hit on the locals. I plan to follow Professor Rogers' advice to enjoy it before we got role assignments because the four days a week we don't have classes will be consumed with practice. I'm fine with that. Today I mostly plan on relaxing and possibly going to the Muse. Instead, I answer the door.

"Hi," Duncan says, "you ready for the big day?"

I look down at my pink and black polka dot Minnie Mouse pyjamas.

"Nope. What exactly is supposed to be happening today?"

"Well I didn't tell you because I wanted it to be a surprise. But Tiana's in my room now with James and I got her to tell me that you had no plans for the days so I decided to make some. Go get dressed and meet me in the lobby."

I do. He's dressed nicely, but casually, in a black button down shirt with the sleeves rolled up to his elbows and I can't help but notice the well fitting jeans. I could vaguely see the outline of his hips and how the denim tightens around his thighs before going in to a straight fit down the rest of his legs. I put on a green dress I got for my cousin's wedding last summer. I think it looks nice and it seems warm out so that and a pair of brown sandals seemed like the best option. I put my hair in a high ponytail and brush my choppy bangs that sit just below my eyebrows.

"So do I get to know where we're going?" I ask as we leave the campus.

"Nope," he says. "Just walk with me."

We talk as we walk along the Thames. I'm starting to notice this is something we will be doing often. I like it. The weather is much better than on the day we met so I'm much happier and feel less like he's going to kidnap me and sell my organs.

"So how often have you been coming to the Globe in the summers?" I ask him.

"This is my third year and I've been coming ever since I began Uni. My parents are from a small town out in Essex. I go back home every now and then but I really don't enjoy it out there. My heart belongs here with the crowds, the culture, and the anonymity."

"How did you find out about the program and that you wanted to do it?" I ask.

"Well, my sister told me. She wants to come too. She's four years younger than me so she can apply next year when she goes to Uni. Until then she's living vicariously through me. She always embraced the arts more than I did. I'm actually a science student."

"Really? I thought you had to be an arts student to come here."

"Nope. I'm finishing up my Chemistry degree soon and then I'm off to medical school. This is just elective credits and because I learned to love it after my first year."

"Where do you want to go to med school?" I ask.

"No idea yet. I'm looking around for schools online but so far nothing fits."

"Well, I'm sure you'll have your choice in schools. You seem really dedicated." His eyes light up when I say this.

"Here we are," Duncan smiles and stretches out his arms. "I knew you were going to see this whole city throughout the duration of the summer but I wanted this to be the first thing you saw. That way you get a preview of what's to come. I swear you can see the whole city from up here." We get in the lineup leading up to the London Eye.

The line - excuse, me, queue - is long but moves quickly. He still decides we need entertainment while we are waiting though.

"So, Olivia… I'm going to name a movie character. Then you have to name another role that movie that the actor or actress also played. First one to run out or take more than a couple of seconds to think about it loses. Here, I'll start with an easy one. Edward Scissorhands."

"The Mad Hatter," I respond.

"Good choice. Sweeney Todd,"

"Victor from *The Corpse Bride*."

"Cry Baby."

"Ichabod Crane."

"Jack Sparrow," Duncan says.

"That's *Captain* Jack Sparrow," I reply.

"Well, I'm afraid you just lost the first round of our game. Hesitate or say something else as a reply instead of an answer to the game, and you lose."

"That's not fair!" I say in fake shock, "you need to say all of the rules to the game before we start."

"Fine, we'll start again," Duncan says.

I'm pretty amazed as to the extent of his film knowledge. He names characters that actors have played in short films or even theatre before they got famous. He completely obliterates me during the game.

I feel a flutter in my chest as I realize the pods don't actually stop to let you on. If you hesitate and miss it going by - albeit slowly, but still moving - the employees get pretty frustrated with you and nearly push you on to the next pod. Before I know it Duncan and I are with twenty strangers on a glass pod looking over London.

"So, what do you think?" Duncan asks as we gaze at the Parliament buildings.

"It's great." I clutch on to the railing.

"Are you afraid of heights?"

"Up until now, no. You know, I've never been in a bubble above a giant river."

"Come here," he chuckles and puts his arms around me to gives me a hug. That's nice. I could do that more. "So you never answered my question before. Do you have a boyfriend back in Canada?"

I'm a little taken aback with his abruptness.

"No, not really."

"Not really? You don't seem very sure of that."

"Well there is a guy at home. And I like him a lot. I'm just not sure if he feels the same way."

"Have you told him how you feel?"

"Yeah. He knows. He's known for a long time." I think about all the time Max and I spent together. I tried to act like all I wanted to be was friends but I knew my real feelings seep through some times. He never acted like he wanted anything more. Granted, he generally bounced from one relationship to the next so he didn't really give me a chance to admit my feelings for him. He sometimes got a little too close to me when he had a girlfriend, and that's how I knew the relationship was doomed. Once or twice I felt like he was hitting on me - buying me a shot at the bar, gently touching my hand at the movies, but I never let it go further than that. I assured myself he wasn't the type of guy to cheat, and I knew I couldn't do that to another girl, even if I hardly knew her. But I guess he knows all about my feelings now.

"Hey look, you can see the Globe from here." I point ahead of us.

"Yeah, I come up here all the time. The tickets aren't too expensive and I love seeing all of London. It's always changing," he says as I see a red double-decker bus cross the bridge.

"Oh yeah right, I owe you for the ticket," I reach for my brown cross body purse.

"No, that's okay. I'm the one who dragged you out here. I have another place to bring you though." We finish up the ride and continued walking. I'm not sure where we're going so just trust and follow him.

My eyes soak in every detail of daily British life that I can. There's a handful of couples that I can clearly pick out as American tourists - all wear white New Balance sneakers, a large camera with a strap around their neck, and slightly - or not so slightly - protruding bellies. I realize it wasn't that long ago when I was as new to this country as they are, and some of those rich old people are probably better travelled than I will ever be. There are posh couples dressed far too formally for the middle of summer, with the women wearing large diamond rings and black stilettos, and sunglasses with some name brand I don't recognize but Tiana probably would. The men are wearing white dress shirts with the sleeves rolled up to their elbows and khaki pants. They look like a knock off Victoria and David Beckham.

"Enjoying the sights?" Duncan asks. We're walking in to a slightly less tourist friendly part of town, the streets lined with no name shawarma places and nail salons.

"Here we are," Duncan says when we approach an underground station.

"Can't we walk above ground?"

"Okay don't tell me you're afraid of both heights and being underground."

"I'm not afraid of being underground. I'm slightly frightened by all the people and what if I get kidnapped. I watch a lot of *Criminal Minds*. Believe me, it's possible I could die under there. There aren't many crowded places back home. I've heard horror stories of the tube."

"Don't worry about it, I'll keep the creeps away."

I carefully descend the staircase with Duncan by my side. He grabs two tube maps from a kiosk in the station. Everything is gloomy and made of cement, which is what I half expect hell to look like. There's a man playing a guitar and singing a Beatles song by the entrance to the trains, one claiming to go east and one claiming to go west. Duncan drops a couple of coins in to the open suitcase and the man nods at him. I open up the map and see a mess of colourful lines that intersect at what seems to be random points.

"That's where we are," Duncan says, "and that's where the Globe is."

"Where are we going?" I ask as we approach the correct train platform.

"That's a surprise," Duncan says.

"Keep away from the yellow line, and mind the gap", I hear an automated women's voice instruct from over the speaker system. I wonder how Duncan can know exactly where he's gong without having to use one of the little folded maps I see on display around the building. Between the different stations and having to know if I should be going North, South, East, or West, I think I would have to get lost at least a couple of times before I figure out where I'm going.

"How long until you were able to get around using the tubes?"

"Like, a week maybe."

I've been in London for that long.

"I was also ten the first time I took them, and didn't go unsupervised until I was sixteen, so I was at an advantage. You'll be able to get around in no time." Duncan squeezes my hand supportively and my heart flutters. I want to be independent and not get lost, but after my first day here, I think that will be easier said than done.

We're surrounded by strangers and we hold on to the handles hanging from the ceiling. A middle aged man and his son, who looked to be about six, squeeze in between Duncan and I. They're wearing red and yellow soccer jerseys with a sports team's crest that I can't place. Duncan playfully banters with them. It's so loud I can only hear parts of the conversation.

"Bloody terrible choice" I hear Duncan say.

"Ah, shut up ya bastard," the father in red punches Duncan on the shoulder. Duncan rustles the little boy's hair, and says something about making his own proper choices when he's older.

I squeeze myself through the couple of people that have found their way between myself Duncan and I and grip the same hand hold he is using.

"Do you know him?" I ask.

"Nope."

"Not to sound weird, but… why were you talking to him?" I have noticed, since I've been here, that with London's huge population, people tend to completely block out everyone else. It's not like everyone in St. John's knows each other, but it's common for people to at least smile as you walk by. I don't think any strangers have acknowledged my presence here unless they want to sell me something. Or unless they're Duncan.

"I see you're not a sports fan. It's football, kind of makes it seem like you know everyone."

"So are you fans of the same team?"

He chuckles. "No, Olivia. I can see you're *really* not a sports fan. My team - Chelsea Football Club," he takes his wallet out of his pocket and shows me. It's worn black leather with a blue lion patch on it, "and their team, Manchester United, are rival teams."

I see the man and his son get off at the next stop, and the little boy offers us a timid wave goodbye as he leaves, his Dad holding his other little fist.

"I see. So you weren't being sarcastic when you said 'bloody terrible choice.'" I say the last bit in the best imitation I can of Duncan. That is, a heavy Essex English accent and very deep.

"And I thought their team choice was bloody awful? Well I mean it is, but that accent. That's a new level of bad."

"Excuse me?" I say in mock offence, "that sounded *exactly* like you."

"My name is Oliviaaaa, and I like reading Shakespeare!" Duncan says in a high pitched valley girl accent, mocking me, "I'm so smart and mysterious because I'm from Canadaaaa," he says with a dramatic wave of his hand.

I see an old man glaring at us from across the tube. By now the the train has emptied enough that Duncan and I are the loudest voices here. Duncan eyes the man, too, and sticks his tongue out at him. Thankfully, this happens just as the tube reaches our stop and we jump out the open doors and start running down the hallway. I reach the escalator first to go back up to ground level and Duncan catches up to me. We stop to catch our breath, clutching our sides from laughing.

"I thought you were supposed to be a footballer," I say, "I didn't think I'd be able to outrun you."

"I," *wheeze,* "watch," *wheeze,* "sports," *wheeze,* "don't", *wheeze,* "play", *wheeze.*

"I can tell," I say, "I'll have to whip you in to shape. We'll go for a run sometime. Maybe next summer you can come to Canada with me and I'll have you trained enough to run a half marathon with me.

"Or…" Duncan says, finally catching his breath, "you can come back to London and we can skip the whole running thing." He shoots me a smile and I shake my head. I hope I have him convinced that he can't make me do anything, but I know if he smiles at me once more I'll turn in to a puddle.

~ ~ ~

"I love coming here. I know it's touristy but I don't care. Today I have you as an excuse to come here," Duncan says as we approach the Tower of London. The thing is massive. Huge beige stone walls tower above us. Guards are dressed in red and black, and I wonder if they're actually trained guards or just for show. I know where I want to go first.

"Can we go to the dungeon?"

"Who do you think I am, Christian Gray?"

"I mean… it's not like…" I feel the heat rise in my cheeks, "I've never even read…"

"I'm kidding!" Duncan says, "I know what you mean and the dungeon is my favourite part. I assumed you would have wanted to see the crown jewels first."

"I still want to see them, just after. I love history and I find medieval torture oddly fascinating. My Father's a war expert and always taught me about the war and punishment methods used by various cultures. You can tell a lot about a group of people based on how they treat those they don't like."

"Huh. Interesting. I wonder if The Muse has any books on war history."

"They do. I already checked. I'll show you a couple of my favourites next time we go together."

"Did you go without me? *Et tu, Brute*," he feigns a stab in the chest and I laugh.

"Yes, I'm sorry. I'm such a traitor. Hopefully there will still be a next time. You know, I hope I didn't offend you too much by not inviting you."

"Nonsense. You seem like the person who was going to do what she wanted regardless of what I insist, and I wouldn't have it any other way."

We look around the room and I'm generally creeped out by the whole thing, which is to be expected. The room is small and dark with remnants of various devices for torture on the wall. There's also a glass panel in the shape of a person to demonstrate how each person would look in the device. It's one thing to read about these types of things but it had a whole different atmosphere in the dungeon, and the creepy music doesn't make the place any more comforting.

We continue on through the tower looking at the education exhibits. Duncan tells me the story of the lost princes while we walk around the grounds.

"The princes were Edward V and Richard of Shrewsbury, Duke of York. They were the sons of Edward IV of England and Elizabeth Woodville. They were 12 and 9 when they went missing in 1483 and they lived here in the Tower. Their Uncle, Richard, Duke of Gloucester was supposed to be looking after them. They were being prepared for Edward's coronation as King but they went missing under the Uncle's care. Most people think the boys were murdered so Richard could take the throne."

"Is that what you believe?"

"I think so. I've done a lot of research on the topic. It's one of the most famous cold cases of all time. I'm kind of obsessed with true crime and mysteries."

"You and Harper must have a lot to talk about then."

"Yeah we do. Harper is a great girl. She's really smart and knows more about criminology than you would expect."

"I like her a lot."

"We dated last summer. She and I have a lot in common."

"You and Harper dated?" I ask, surprised.

"Yeah. She or Tiana didn't tell you?"

"Nope. I mean I wouldn't expect them to, it didn't really come up."

"Yeah I guess so."

"Why didn't you guys stay together?"

"We lived too far apart to make it work. We tried the long distance thing but it only lasted like a month after she went back to the US."

"The long distance thing would be really hard." I can't let myself fall for this guy. I can't be another summer fling for him. So I've decided it. Duncan and I are just going to be friends and that's it.

The last stop we make is to see the crown jewels. I didn't want to seem like the stereotypical girl going gaga over something sparkly but they really were a sight to see. We walked through a room explaining the history of the jewels and what each piece meant. The jewels themselves were of course stunning. I can't believe something so beautiful occurred in nature and it was only human who found it, not created it. I make a mental note to pick up a book on geology later.

We leave the Tower and take the tube back, it's much less crowded this time of day. I had a great day with Duncan and have to keep reminding myself that he is off-limits. I don't need to be romantically involved with anyone right now anyway, I know school will keep my busy enough. I look over at one of the benches and the man sitting on it looks back at me and I feel my stomach come up in my throat. For a good three seconds, I think it's him. I think Michael is here, in London, following me. Then I remember that there's no way he could be here. Not after the accident.

"I need to go to the washroom. I'll just be a sec," I say when we approach the washrooms in the tube station. I'm starting to feel anxious and my hands are shaking. I've felt this before, and it's not the anxiety from being up high or underground. I thought I was done with this.

"I hardly think you're going to take a shower in there."

"Excuse me?"

"Toilet. We call it a toilet."

"Ew."

"You're not fooling anyone by calling it a washroom. You're not washing anything - except your hands, hopefully."

I don't have time for banter with Duncan right now. I try to hide my anxiety but quickly go in to the washroom and I'm glad to see it's empty. It's not the first time I've done this in a public washroom, but I still cringe when I bring my face close to the bowl of the toilet and stick my index finger in the back of my throat. I try and fail to keep my breakfast down. I didn't eat much this morning, so I'm done quickly. I clean myself up and use some of the mouthwash I always keep in a travel sized container in my purse. I blot the sweat off my forehead. I'm not sure what drove me to do it again this time, but I know it won't happen again. At least until I get home. I won't do it again while I'm here.

I root around in my messenger bag and look for something to use to freshen up. I have to hurry or Duncan will start to wonder what is going on. I don't have a toothbrush, but I have some gum. I swish water in my mouth and spit it out before chewing the gum. I run my fingers through my hair, trying the dry the sweat in my roots. I touch up my makeup, and decide that will have to be good enough for now.

We leave the tube station and begin our walk back down the Thames. The air has gotten cooler since we walked up, and it's a good break from the heat of all the bodies in the tube. We pass a news stand, which seems to be giving by the day updates on the royal baby. The Duchess of Cambridge is pregnant with her first born baby and the excitement seems to be all that everyone is talking about.

"I hope the baby is a girl," I say. What do you think it will be?

"I don't know what but I hope it's a boy."

"No, girls are way better. Can you imagine all the cute dresses she'll be put in for events? Adorable."

"Being a Princess is more than pretty dresses."

"Yeah but you have a democracy, too. The royal family doesn't do much, do they?"

"Maybe not when it comes to the law, but they are still held to a high standard. I know you have never grown up in this culture, but remember that it is a different culture than yours. No one can really understand how much that baby girl would have to go through."

"I don't get it though. It's 2013. She won't have to be married off to the Prince of another country to make an ally."

"No, but they'll still act like she will. She will have to go to a lot of additional training so she can go to events. I almost feel bad for the Duchess, except she agreed to marry in to it. It would be hard for her to conform to their standards but she is actually doing a fair job of it right now. The baby doesn't have a choice."

"But what's the worst that would happen? They can't force her to do those things."

"No, but if she didn't it would ruin her reputation. She still doesn't have a choice."

"Maybe."

"So would you want to do that? Be in the spotlight all the time?"

"Oh hell no."

He raises an eyebrow at my abruptness.

"I'm an introvert. Being in the media sounds like actual hell."

"So there's nothing that would make you talk to the media?"

I think about it.

"Nope, probably not."

"So what's the difference between that and perfuming on stage?"

"Because when I'm on stage it's different. I know it's crazy, but it feels like it's just me hanging out in my room with my friends and pretending to be different characters. It's like an out of body experience, I guess."

"Huh. That's a pretty good reason."

"Why do you perform?"

"It's in my blood. My parents did it, so now I do. Eventually my sister will, too. Also I'm a pretty big fan of all the attention. What was your first performance?"

"I was Cindy Loo in my elementary school's Christmas play. It was my big debut."

"And how did it go? A standing ovation, I assume."

"Not quite. I got nervous and puked on stage. They had to pull the curtains really quickly to clean it up. I didn't have a backup costume so I finished the show in my gym clothes and slightly smelling like vomit. It was gross."

"That sounds traumatizing," he says laughing.

"My Mom still brought me flowers and took me out for a Happy Meal after the show, so all in all I would say it was a pretty successful day."

"I love how casual you are about puking on stage."

"They show must go on," I say, and fling my arms out dramatically.

———————————

Chapter Seven

Some Cupid kills with arrows, some with traps - Much Ado About Nothing, William Shakespeare

    Tiana and I sit in The Muse, each with a cup of coffee in front of us.

    "So tell me all about the date," she says.

    "Okay it was *so* not a date."

    "Tell me exactly what happened and I will determine whether or not it was a date."

    "He took me on a surprise trip to the Eye. We went on a great ride and we both learned I am afraid of heights. On the way home we went to the tower of London and then got ice cream on the way home. That's all."

"Did he pay for it?" She asks.

"Yes. Because he's a great friend. I did not need to expect him to pay for it. I'm sure I'll pay for the next date."

"Right. So you just said it was a date."

I look down at the floor.

"So what about this Max guy at home? Are you still into him?"

"Yes. Very much so. And he responded to my last message so maybe he likes me too. I mean I knew he would be busy this summer, he's taking a full course load so he can graduate early."

"A guy doesn't forget for two weeks to text back the girl he likes. All you two did was hook up, I'm sure it meant nothing to him."

"Talking to you always makes me feel *so* much better."

"Well I speak the truth. You need to forget about this other guy and look at what is right in front of you."

"I guess so. But I think I just want to make it through this trip and enjoy the location and the work. I don't need to meet a guy here to have a good time."

"But it certainly makes it more fun."

"There's someone back home you should meet. You and Jenna would be great friends."

"I would like nothing more than to meet your friends and find new ways to conspire against you."

"The two of you would most definitely do a lot of that."

~ ~ ~

"I can't believe we've been here two weeks already," Harper says the next morning at breakfast.

"I know. And we haven't even done anything super fun yet. We have to go out before the craziness of role announcements and rehearsal," Tiana says.

"I'm sure we'll be busy but won't we still have some free time?" I ask.

"For normal people like me, yes. But I know the three of you," Tiana looks pointedly at Harper, James and I. "Will be obsessive about practicing. For good reason. I mean I love you all but you both need a lot of help. Besides, you've already been studying and practicing for auditions. You need to go out to the pubs at least a couple of times while you're here."

"She speaks the truth," Duncan agrees.

"Okay, fine. We'll do something tonight. It's Friday so I can't see why we shouldn't go out now," I say.

"Great," Tiana lights up and smiles at Duncan and I. I ignore her as I take a bite out of my apple.

~ ~ ~

So what's the plan? I text Tiana as my last class is ending.

Well I've been planning it all day so get ready.

We disperse back to our respective rooms to get dressed. Tiana puts on her favourite pop playlist and curls my hair. I tell her my hair is so naturally straight it can't hold a curl. She insists that I am just doing it wrong. Apparently she's great at hair and makeup as well as fashion because the spray she uses in my hair makes it keep its shape all night. She gives me a bold red lip and just some natural looking eye makeup with a bit of mascara. I put on a flowy black dress with cap sleeves.

Tiana is dressed up much fancier than I am. She's wearing a tight silver dress with a plunging neckline. She chose with a glossy pink lipstick and a dark purple eye that goes out into a cat eye shape. I think that much makeup would make me feel like a clown but she wears it with pride and it looks stunning on her.

We go downstairs to the lobby to meet with the others. Harper is dressed simply as usual, in jeans and a pink button down top with a pair of pink ballet flats. James is wearing his usual uniform of black jeans, a black t-shirt and a black leather jacket. Duncan looks more dressed up than he usually is. He is also in black jeans but with a white dress shirt with a blue jacket on top and he even had on a blue bow-tie. I laugh when I see it.

"What? Bow ties are cool," he says.

I have to agree.

We make our way to The Crown. It's small and packed, some people are our age and playing cards or just drinking and having a good time, some are older and playing darts or pool.

James walks up to the two men at the bar and gives them each a big bear hug, and so does Duncan. I have a feeling they frequent this place.

We get to the counter and Tiana orders a cider. I ask for the same.

We take our drinks to an empty table and I wearily take my first a sip of the cider. It's great, and fruity and carbonated. It could be a little bit sweeter for my taste but I think I can get used to it.

"Do you know them well?" I ask the boys and look over to the men at the bar.

"They're Ty and Colin. Great guys, just got married last summer. They opened up the pub a few years ago. We come here often, you could say they like the business the Globe kids bring them," James says. They seem nice. I'm really starting to like all the people I am meeting here. I realize how much I am going to miss all of this when I g\et home, I was starting to form a community and a family with the people here.

We laugh and have a good time for a couple of pints. Once Tiana decides we were sufficiently buzzed she insists we make our way to the nightclub.

The club is close by. I can hear the bass pumping from down the road. We're walking up to the building when Tiana explains the history of the building and why it didn't look like the clubs I was used to.

"English people really liked to build churches back in the day, but having a million churches in every town just wasn't feasible at a certain point. So they needed to find a new use for them. The way they had them designed was kind of funny, too. There was just a big open space with no pews and people used to stand at the services. Eventually they were used as buildings for dances and other recreational events. Now, they're clubs. They call it a Rave in the Nave."

"That's amazing," I laugh.

We walk up the steps to the building that of course, looks like a huge church, except for the vibrations radiating from it and I can see strobe lights coming from some of the windows and a purple light dancing around some of the others.

We walk up to the bar and James insists on buying us a round of shots. I'm not much of a drinker except for the odd glass of wine in the evenings so I have to slow down in comparison to everyone else. After two shots of vodka and three drinks of red bull and vodka, I retire myself to water and can feel myself loosen as I dance in a circle with my friends, and a couple of other people we don't know. A guy across the circle from me meets my gaze. I feel a flush as his brown eyes hold mine a little too long and I look down at my drink. Tiana nudges me in my right side and I try to ignore her.

I'm not a great dancer but I'm a pro in comparison to Duncan. I'm not sure if it's because he had a couple too many drinks or if he's always this uncoordinated but his dance moves somehow involved flailing his arms in opposite directions. I laugh and try to imitate his dance moves. Tiana, Harper, and James get tired and leave just after 2 am. Duncan and I decide to stay because he knows how to get home and has sobered up a little bit. Eventually we are there so late the music slows down and the bar stops serving.

~ ~ ~

I know Tiana will be sleeping when I get home but she wakes up as soon as I open the door.

"Tell me what happened," she insists.

"I'm tired," I say as I change into pyjamas.

"I still want to hear all about it." I shut the bathroom door to take off my makeup and brush my teeth.

"So you haven't gotten out of telling me. Did he kiss you?"

"No, we did not kiss," I say.

"Well, what exactly happened?"

"We just danced, that's all."

"Did you want him to kiss you?" she asked.

"Yeah, of course I did," I kind of don't want to talk about it right now. I had a good night and don't want to over analyze it but I know Tiana won't let that happen. I know I want to be with Duncan but I still have Max at home to think about. I doubt I could do the long distance thing. I still have two years left of school and god even knows where he would be going for medical school next year. I know I can't hold him back by asking him to go to my University for med school, he has so many options. Most of which aren't even in Canada. Besides, that's looking too far into the future. I don't want to hold myself back either. Who knows who I would meet throughout the duration of my University career.

"What about Max?" She asks.

"I don't know. I don't want to talk about it," I say before falling asleep.

~ ~ ~

We're all feeling pretty crappy the next morning at breakfast. Tiana and I don't roll out of bed until almost noon. I didn't drink as much as everyone else but the sight of bacon and eggs turns my stomach. Instead I decide to make my way down to The Muse and grab a coffee and maybe a scone.

I go up to their selection and pick up *Dubliners* by James Joyce. I decide to read some European authors now while I'm here. The black coffee is agreeing with my stomach so I go back for a lemon cranberry scone and another cup of coffee.

"Did you have any before you got here?" Nick, the barista at The Muse asks.

"No I didn't, so I think I'm entitled at least three more cups after this one," I say.

"Make that three cups including this one, and you've got yourself a deal," Nick says and pours me up another cup. Nick is the barista that works here the most. Once he found how exactly how much coffee I can consume in the run of a day, he has put me on a strict four coffees limit. He says that any more than that, and the stress of going to school will kill me at twenty-five. I know he's training to be a nutritionist, but I think he stretched the truth for that one.

I get back to my table and continue reading when Fleur and her clones walk in.

"I can't believe Duncan is with that Canadian girl *Elle est grossiére*," Fleur says.

"Are they serious or just hooking up?" Rosie asks.

"I don't know but he's way too hot to mess around with someone like her. That girl is going to be a one summer wonder. I know she won't be back next year," Fleur replies.

"I heard she had a boyfriend back home. What if she's cheating on him," Mary says.

"I doubt she could get two guys. I mean look at the girl, she does not have the look to perform here. She's much too plain," Fleur says with a wave of her hand.

"She needs to get back to her books, seriously. Did you see her at the club with Duncan last night? If she does have a boyfriend at home, she's cheating on him. She dances like a total slut. I wish I could find out who he was and let him know. That would show that bitch, thinking she can just come up here and steal your role," Cathy says.

"What exactly makes you think she'll get the role?" Fleur asks, clearly getting mad.

"She's here on a scholarship. She has to be half good."

"Oh no. She won't get any role if I have anything to say about it."

I can't believe what I'm hearing. My table is in the back of the cafe, hidden behind a bookshelf. I like it here because it means I can get away from the hectic campus and dress of classes and seeing the same people every day but having to Fleur and her clones talk about me and my choices makes me furious. I already know I won't like Fleur but I don't need her and her clones making fun of who I choose to spend my time with. Part of me wants to confront her on what she was saying about me but I decide to wait and see if it gets any worse.

~ ~ ~

Everyone is buzzing at breakfast the next day. Today is the day when the play will be announced.

"I heard it's *Cymbeline*," one of Fleur's clones says to the other.

"Not it's not. They did that one only two years ago. It's going to be *Love's Labour's Lost*."

"No, stupid, they're doing that one professionally this year. They wouldn't have two productions of the same show."

"Would you three please shut up. None of you know what you're talking about," Fleur snaps at them.

"What's wrong with the big, bad wolf this morning?" I ask Harper .

"Everything."

"Fleur's super nervous when it comes to performing," Tiana whispers.

"I thought she loves it," I say

"She does but her parents are strict. They're both doctors and expected her to go to med school, or at least law school. She wanted to go to school for visual arts and took a couple theatre classes as an elective. She found out she was good at it and had the look that movies want. She would rather perform on stage but she convinced her parents to accept her on film."

"Film and commercials are where the money is so her parents gave her ten years to make it big on film or they were going to cut her off," Harper says.

"So now she needs to make it big on stage within the next few years so she can make it without them," Tiana says.

"I think she's going to give up and marry rich," I can tell Harper really does not like this girl. I need to change the subject.

"So, guys, I need your help with Max," I'm with just Harper and Tiana so I feel like I can talk about Max without it being weird around Duncan.

"Has he texted you back yet?" Harper asks.

"Yeah, actually. I've messaged him like four times since we slept together. But then a while ago he texted back saying he would see me when I get back."

"That's good, right? If he didn't like you at all then he just wouldn't have said anything." Harper says.

"No way," Tiana says, "he's best friends with your best friend's boyfriend. He probably doesn't want you to have feelings for him but also doesn't want to be a total dick to you. If he did that he knows that Jenna will hate him and he won't be able to spend as much time with Steven by default. I still think he's bad news."

"How has he been to your friends back home? I wonder if there's something going on with him that you just don't know about," Harper says. I make a mental note to call Jenna later this evening.

We finish up breakfast and made it over to the Globe.

Marcus is standing on the stage in a dramatic pose. I wouldn't doubt he came out of the womb singing some song from *Rent*.

"Okay, okay, sit down on the benches and pay attention. I have gathered you all here today for a very special occasion. I just wanted to let you all know that this year we will be performing, for the first time ever by you students, *The Merchant of Venice*."

We all clap and cheer. I've never read this one before so I'm really excited to get to know it better.

He hands out the scripts and has a few people get up on stage and recite some lines. We're told that this is in no way was this actually the audition, but it was good to get each of us up on stage and get used to some of the lines. Tiana and I run a couple of lines together and have a lot of fun. I feel a lot less nervous for the audition after that because I felt like I knew what they were expecting.

~ ~ ~

I'm pacing up and down the hallway waiting for my turn to audition. The order of students is going alphabetically so I go last. The curse of the W last name. I continue pacing as I reread the script. I still hold it in my hands even though I have all the lines memorized. I know some other students almost race each other to get off script and are really proud of themselves when they reach that point. I don't. I find it really comforting to hold the words in my hand even when I could make it without.

About five minutes before I'm about to go on I hear a voice around the corner.

"You know I need that lead," a female's voice says, and I can hear a French accent in it. Is that Fleur? That has to be her.

"I know you do but I can't make it look like you're my favourite," I hear a man's voice say.

"But I am your favourite," she says flirtatiously and I hear a kissing noise.

"I already gave you the script and what we're looking for. You rocked the audition. It will be easy for you to get the role anyway."

"Oh, come on. Giving me that script wasn't a help. Everyone knows what we're performing and has read it by now. The small changes you've made won't matter. I need a guarantee I have the part."

"Well, you know what I have in mind. Keep with our arrangement and I know you'll have it. I might give you a little extra next time."

"You better or I'll have to take my services elsewhere. You know how in demand I am."

"No one has the connections I have. You need me."

"Whatever. I can make it in this town without you."

"So you don't want the lead? You know I can get it for you."

"Of course I want it. At the end of the summer we'll look at where we are and see if I need or want to renew our contract. If things go as planned this summer I won't need you to get me any further."

"Okay. And until the contract is up, I'll see you at the usual time and place," Just as he finishes the conversation Mrs. Storm comes out of the audition room as I hear the squeak on the floor as Fleur spins around and the clack of her heels pounding down the hallway.

"Olivia, we're ready for you," I walk in and looked at the panel of professionals in front of me. There are four seats, one of which was empty after Mrs. Storm, the head of the acting department sits back down. The others are occupied by Mr. Howlett, the head of the music department, and Mrs. Wagner, the head of casting. As I'm getting ready to begin, Mr. Barnes walks in.

"Sorry I'm late. Had to take a quick break," he says.

I walk up to shake the hands of the people there.

"Sorry I'm yet to meet you outside of class, Olivia. I hear you're a very promising student and I'm excited to see you perform," Mr. Barnes says. In the same voice I heard out in the hallway. I try to clear Fleur and Mr. Barnes from my mind and recite what I have prepared.

"If the dull substance of my flesh were thought,

Infurious Distance should not stop my way;

For then despite of space I would be brought,

From limits far remote, where thou dost stay.

No matter then although my foot did stand

Upon the farthest earth removed from thee;

For nimble thought can jump both sea and land

As soon as think the place where he would be.

Bu ah! Thought kills me that I am not thought,

To leap large lengths of miles when thou arts gone,

But that, so much of earth and water rought, I must attend time's leisure with my moan,

> Receiving nought by elements so slow

> But heavy tears, badges of either's woe."

The judges don't react when I finish, just make some scribbles down on their notebooks and tell me I can leave. I feel fairly confident with my audition. I just know I'm excited to get home and talk about what had happened with Tiana. Finally, I can think about something besides Max and figure out what Fleur is up to.

"Hey, how'd the audition go?" Tiana asks.

"The audition itself was fine but I overheard something interesting I wanted to talk to you about."

"Oh I am *so* listening."

"Well first I overheard a conversation with Fleur and her clones in The Muse saying horrible things about me. She didn't know I was there. Then I overheard a conversation with what seemed to be Fleur and Mr. Barnes"

"Go on," she pushes.

"They were talking about something really secretively so I couldn't hear well. But she said she needed his help to make sure she got the lead role, something about a contract lasting the summer, and I heard a what sounded like them kissing."

"That's ridiculous. She's totally sleeping with him to get the part," Tiana says.

"That's what I was thinking but I didn't want to just say it," I say. Tiana is always more outspoken than I was so I knew she would confirm my suspicions.

"We have to figure out what they're doing."

"Yeah. I can't just let her get away with this. This is totally wrong," I wanted that lead too and I deserve it just as much as she does.

"We can't just up and ask either of them. They'll just lie and either get more secretive or stop what they're doing all together. I know we want them to stop but if he's sleeping with the actors that's wrong and the management at the theatre needs to do something about him."

"We need a plan," I say. We immediately start brainstorming what we can do.

Chapter Eight

> Though this be madness, yet there is method in't - Hamlet, William Shakespeare

Duncan and I sit next to each other and just barely hold hands. My hand is gently placed on top of his, so I can feel his warm skin against mine, but if someone looks our way we can quickly undo it. I don't want Tiana to see that we are getting close. I love her and trust her but I know she likes to gossip and I want to keep what Duncan and I might have together our secret for now.

Marcus walks on to the stage and everyone falls silent.

"The judges were very impressed with how you all did on your auditions and they want you to know that this was a very hard choice to make. You've all improved since last year or have come here for the first time with an arsenal of skills in your belt. But anyway, I'll just get to what you're all here for," I squeeze Duncan's hand.

"Shylock will be played by Duncan Doyle…" I smile at him and hear Tiana gasp dramatically next to me, "… Bassanio will be played by James Johnson, Jessica will be played by Olivia Williams, and Portia will be played by Fleur LeClerc".

Tiana and I exchange a knowing glance. I'm generally pleased with the results. I knew I wouldn't get the lead role in my first year and I'm fine with that. But if Fleur only got it because she slept her way to the top then I am not fine with *that*. Now that the roles have been announced and we know we have a possible bad situation on our hands, we can put the plan into action.

Tiana and I walk silently into our room.

"We need to do something," she says as soon as we close the door.

"I know. But we're not exactly detectives. It won't be easy to find information. If there even is anything to find. Who knows, maybe she just got it because she's the best."

"No. I know her and I know how she does in auditions. She lands stuff based on the previous work she gets. It was always a mystery to everyone how she got so much work when she always choked so badly in auditions. She puts too much pressure on herself and it back fires on her," she says. Tiana had been her best friend and roommate so she must know what she is talking about.

"I don't want to jump to any conclusions," I say. "First I want to gather some information and make sure what we're doing and thinking is right."

"So you want to stalk her."

"Essentially, yes."

"Then we'll need the assistance of a professional," Tiana begins furiously typing on her computer. I know right away who that will be.

In a matter of minutes Harper is in our room and Tiana is giving her a summary of what I had heard and what we thought of it. Harper's Mom is the head detective in her hometown and Harper often helps her after school. She has been on stake-outs as a kid when her Mom couldn't find childcare when she needed to leave at a moment's notice. In addition to that she had grown up on *Nancy Drew* books and considered herself a pretty talented sleuth. She is going to be the brains of this whole operation.

"Do we know which room is her's?" Harper asks.

"Yes. It's on our floor, the last one on the right hand side of the hallway," I say.

"Good. I thought so since I haven't seen her on second, which you know is the other girls floor. Also she is next to the window in the hallway which means there is a little seating area right next to her door. No one really uses it but one of you can sit there with a book or homework or something and hang out without being really suspicious. I expect you both to do this at different times, randomly though, not on a schedule so she doesn't catch on. And never at the same time because you geniuses are likely to talk about her when you don't know she's in the room. The walls are thin here so she'll hear you for sure. You also have me who you can text at any time and have me wait by the elevator or front door to see where she's going at any time."

"Oh my god we are so creepy," I say.

"Are you dropping out of the mission?" Harper asks. I think about how hard I worked to get here and how much I need to make sure I didn't miss out on the role because Fleur is good in bed.

"No way."

"Then listen to me and we'll get started soon."

~ ~ ~

The plan begins with me stationed in the sitting area at the end of the hallway by Fleur's room. I thought a steak-out would be more interesting but it's mostly me with my laptop open writing a paper for my fashion history course. Fleur doesn't come or go for the two hours I am sitting there. I send a text to Tiana:

It's your turn. I need to rehearse in the room.

Fine, I'll be there soon. Don't leave before I get there or we'll miss something.

I'm highly skeptical that we were going to miss much of anything, but I comply. After practicing in my room for a while I decide that I'm not going to get anywhere just going over my lines in front of the mirror. A couple minutes later I find myself back over at the Globe and knocking on Mr. Barnes' door.

"Hello, Olivia. Come in," he says as he lets me in.

"Hey, um, I'm having some problems with my tone of voice in a couple of these lines and I was just wondering if you could help me pinpoint where I'm going wrong."

"Yeah, of course. Why don't you start by letting me see where you are."

I begin with a few lines from one of my scenes.

"You could really be adding more drama there in the first bit. And soften your voice as you cue the next actor."

"Okay, that's great. I'll try that."

"And..." he walks up to me. "Just let me feel what you're doing with your diaphragm here," he places one had on my stomach and another on the small of my back as I recite the lines again.

"That's really great," he keeps his hands in place. I wiggle out of his grasp.

"By the way, Mr. Barnes. I thought I did really well on my audition. I was just wondering what I could do better next time to get a better part," I ask.

"Well, Olivia, I'm glad you asked. You did do very well but there are some places in which you can improve. I would like to get you to that place so you'll be better prepared next year. Come see me more often and I'm sure you'll be up to the level of someone like, say, Fleur LeClerc."

"Okay, thanks for all the help. I'm sure I'll be back to practice more."

"It's no problem, really. Please drop by any time," he says as he sits back down at his desk.

That was weird. I had assumed he was a little creepy if he really was sleeping with Fleur but asking me to be more like her is a whole new level. I would never choose to do something like that. I get back to the room and call Jenna on the campus's land line. I'm glad that Tiana is still on steak-out duty so she wasn't in the room.

"Okay, tell me everything that happened," Jenna says when I tell her about the experience I just had.

"First it was all normal. Then he kind of touched my stomach and back and said something about seeing where I take my breaths. I mean I know music teachers will do that when people are singing but I've never had someone do that before. And then when I finished he just kept his hands there until I moved away."

"I really don't want you to go back there," she says.

"I need to. I need to find out if Fleur is paying him for the roles. And I need help, this performance has to be good and he's the director. I'm stuck with him for the summer whether I like it or not."

"He's still really creepy and I don't like him."

"I know, but what other choice do I have? Besides, I probably just took it the wrong way. He knows he can't sleep with his students, especially more than one, and keep his job."

"I don't know but I just want you to come home soon," she says solemnly.

"What's going on with you? I can tell something's wrong."

"I didn't want to have you worry about me when you have so much going on, and I really want you to enjoy your trip," she says.

"Well now I know there's something wrong so you *have* to tell me."

"Fine. Something's up with Steven."

"Is he okay?"

"I guess so."

"What do you mean you guess so?"

"He's kind of… stopped talking to me since you left."

"Why?"

"We were talking about you and Max and got into a bit of a fight. I mean I didn't think Max should have slept with you if he didn't plan on at least trying to be with you."

"And how did that make him mad at you?"

"Well, he said that he knew Max was going to do that for a while. And he didn't think that what Max did was wrong."

"Wait, he thinks that sleeping with me and then not talking to me is okay?"

"Apparently."

"So you guys are fighting over this?"

"Well… we're kind of broken up now." I hear Jenna's voice crack.

"I'm so sorry," I say.

"Me too."

"I mean you don't have to defend me. Maybe he'll come to his sense and you'll get back together in a little while, you never know."

"Thanks but I don't think that's going to happen. I'm glad I told you though. I wanted to keep it from your for at least a little while but I feel better now that I have told you."

I'm the only one who has a class with Fleur so I have to figure out where she goes after that. I follow her as best as I can while still keeping it incognito. I'm sure Harper would have done a better job than me with the being stealthy thing but I'm the only option for this part of the plan.

I get a text from Harper :

I have a change of plans, no more stake out. We need more drastic measures. We're going to need to break into a room. Meet me in my room in 10.

Uh, oh. Breaking into a room sounds illegal.

Harper's room is plain, except for a batman poster above her bed. She has one of the few single rooms in the Commons.

"I used my sleuthing skills and landed us the big daddy," Harper says.

"Please continue," Tiana says and takes a bite of a powdered donut from the package on her lap. She offers me one. I almost take it before I remember the cheese danish I had at breakfast, and imagine it's half a day's worth of calories so I refuse the donut.

"Okay, so at work today I spent most of my time trying to come up with a reason to get in to the file room." Harper works a couple of hours a week in the marketing department of the program office.

"And?" I ask.

"And, I got one. They gave Jane, you know, that tour guide I'm friends with? Anyway, they gave her the key and the door code. I explained what we are doing, and as long as we don't snitch, we have the night to get in there and do whatever we need to do, and leave the place seemingly untouched. So we need to leave right now. I have my phone, I can take pictures of any evidence we find. But we need to leave right now and we can go investigate the files to see if they have anything on Fleur. I would have just asked Jane to look earlier but that's not really her department, so I couldn't."

I look at Tiana and Harper. "Let's do it."

We go down to the file room and Harper unlocks the door, and quickly puts in the key code so no one hears it beeping. We enter the big concrete room with files from floor to ceiling.

"How am I supposed to know which one is her's?"

"Because Jane looked it up earlier. Everyone has a computer generated student number, which Jane can search for in the work database by searching her name and seeing what the number is. And I have it right here." She holds up a pink sticky note with a string of numbers on it.

"Perfect."

We find her student file, pull it out, and sit on the floor to go through it. There are lots of transcripts and reference letters. It all seems pretty average, until we get to the things from last year.

July 17, 2012: 3:34 PM

To: Cassie Anderson, head of Human Resources

From: Amy Ward, student number 24028

Hello Ms. Anderson,

My name is Amy Ward, and I have debated writing this email or not for some time, and I have decided it is in the best interest in terms of safety of the Globe's students and faculty. While I was outside the campus, I saw someone who I am sure is Fleur LeClerc go up to an apartment building not far from our theatre, and be greeted at the door by the director, Mr. Barnes. I find it extremely suspicious as to why she would be going to his apartment after hours if he has an office on campus that students can utilize when they need extra help. I hope nothing is happening between them, but I'm afraid he might be showing some favouritism to certain students.

Thank you for your time,

Amy Ward.

July 25, 2012: 8:17 AM

To: Amy Ward, student number 24028

From: Cassie Anderson, Head of Human Resources

Thank you for your concern Ms. Ward. I have spoken to both of the accused, and at this time they both deny the claims. We are not choosing to involve the legal authorities as we have no proof any illegal activity has occurred. We will continue to investigate this claim, but for the time being we think your concern is superfluous.

Sincerely,

Cassie Anderson

July 19, 2012: 1:47 PM

To: Fleur LeClearc, student number, 45204

From: Cassie Anderson, Head of Human Resources

Hello Ms. LeClerc,

I would like to bring to your attention a concern that was brought to me in the past few days. I have been informed by another student that you have been seen outside of Mr. Barnes' apartment complex. If this was you, I would like to remind you that it is inappropriate for students to see a professor off campus and outside of his/her office hours.

July 19, 2012: 2:05 PM

To: Cassie Anderson, Head of Human Resources

From: Fleur LeClearc, student number, 45204

No, that was not me.

August 15, 2012

This legally binding document hereby declares that the accused Richard Evan Barnes (please print) is recounting his/her account of the event in question. The accused will recount his/her events as he/she remembers them, and sign and date on the provided space below.

I asked Fleur LeClerc to come to my apartment to practice after hours with the intention of having sex with her. She consented to everything that happened and she was an adult at the time of our interaction. I do not think what I did was right, but I did not commit any crimes. It only happened once, and I regret the one time it happened, and will never do it again.

Richard Evan Barnes (name)   *August 30, 2012* (date)

This legally binding document hereby declared that Richard Evan Barnes will have to comply with the following legal requirements:

1) Have no physical contact with the victim and her area of work, living, and/or education.

2) Not have any verbal contact with Fleur LeClerc, or any other students, off campus and/or outside office hours.

3) Take a course on sexual harassment in the workplace and complete all required paperwork to coincide with said class.

If either of these legal requirements are not met, The Globe has the right to terminate Mr. Barnes' employment and further pursue legal action.

"That. Fucking. Bitch." I say to break the silence.

"She slept with her teacher. That's awful, that poor girl must feel so abused," Harper says.

"No, she's a slut. I hate her. Always hated her. Wait Harper, do you remember when Barnes was off for the end of the summer last year? This must have been why. He told us he broke a rib. Fucking liar," Tiana says.

"You used to be best friends with her," Harper says.

"Yeah, well... never mind."

~ ~ ~

I discover that Harper knows a lot about detective work but it is both not as fun as I had expected, and not as easy as I had expected. Fleur doesn't do much besides hang out in her room and gossip with her clones. I decide we need to get into her room. And while we were at it, we have to get into Barnes' office, too. This thought brought me to the room of someone I don't know well but I know he has a way with technology.

"Olivia? I didn't expect to see you here?" I hear Kenneth say when he opens his campus room door. I have a couple of classes with him and he mentioned once that he was a computer science student who mostly does studio and light work. Everything he says sounds like a question. I know I have to get in and out of here as quickly as I can, so other people don't get suspicious from seeing us randomly spending time together.

"I need a favour from you. It's pretty important but I don't want anyone to know that I'm here," he looks at me like I'm crazy but gestures for me to come in. I sit down at the small table with two chairs. I'm glad his roommate isn't here so we don't have to ask him to leave.

"So what's going on?" he asks.

"I've been having some problems with some of the people here. Most everyone is great, except I think a couple of people are out to get me. I can't let that happen, and it's not something I can tell administration about. But I need eyes and ears in two rooms, I need the equipment and instructions on how to get them set up."

"I can do that. I don't even want to know what you're using it for, as long as you can promise me it's nothing malicious," he says.

I think about what he said for a moment.

"It's just justice and other people owning up to what they've done. I don't plan on being discovered, but if I do, I promise your name will never come up. I'll say we bought everything online and it came with instructions."

"Sounds good. One more thing though? Can you… ask your friend, Harper, to go out with me sometime?" I can't believe what I'm hearing. Kenneth suddenly goes from annoying to the most adorable person on the planet. The genius and the sleuth. *I love it.*

"I can ask her, but I can't guarantee anything. She may not want to go, which I can't control, but I'm sure she'll at least go out for coffee if I ask and if she has time," I say.

"Thank you. I know she doesn't know me well, but I thought we might have fun together, you know?"

I explain to him what I need and he says he would search around to see where he can get it for the cheapest price, and I leave.

Chapter Nine

Did my heart love till now? Forswear it, sight! For I ne'er saw true beauty till this night - Romeo and Juliet, William Shakespeare

My computer beeps with a video call from Jenna.

"I have best news," she says.

"Well I could use some. Hit me."

"Dad is flying to London and he's going to be there for four days. I can come see you," she says.

"That's amazing. I can't wait. When are you coming?" I ask.

"At the end of the summer, the last week of August. I know you perform August 27 so I'm going to make absolutely sure I can visit my very best friend on that day and watch you make history."

"You're sweet, but it's really not that big of a deal. I have a minor role so I won't get the contract, and I likely won't be back next semester. You know the scholarship I got is only for people coming for the first time."

"I know you'll get one next year, too. There are more scholarships and you're the most talented girl they have. Anyway, let's not talk about that right now, making plans is way more fun. I only have three nights for us to tear up the city." Jenna and I make plans for her time here for a little while before she has to go. I'm glad we get to do some talking so I can make sure she's okay with the breakup and me not being there for her. I feel better knowing she will be in London soon, and I can show her the city I have fallen so deeply in love with.

I don't think it's just London that I've fallen in love with. My heart nearly stops every time I think about Duncan and how supportive he has been with me in all of this. I never thought that someone would love me after I had been sexually assaulted or harassed, which is why I never told Jenna or Max about Michael. They'll think I'm crazy or that I was some kind of slutty kid. No, I can't let that happen. Even if Duncan is being nice to me now, that can still change. I know it can and I don't want it to. I can't tell him about Michael.

I decide to go up to Harper's room to talk to her about Kenneth.

"I have a slightly weird proposition for you," I say when I sit down on her bed. She raises an eyebrow at me. "So you know Kenneth, that tech guy?"

"The tall one with the red hair and green eyes?" She asks me.

"Yeah, him. I told him what we needed from him with the plan and he kind of asked me for a favour. From you."

"Go on," she says with caution.

"He wants to go out with you. Now, before you answer, know that he already agreed to help us out and not ask questions. I told him I could ask you for your help but that I couldn't guarantee anything because that would be weird. But he seems to really like you, so if you said yes, maybe just coffee or something, not even a big time commitment…" I don't know why I'm so nervous, probably because I haven't played cupid for anyone before. I'm not sure what protocol is. If she says no, would I have to tell him? Oh god, what if he starts crying?

"I'll do it," she says.

"Really?" I beam with excitement.

"Yeah. He seems nice. I have class with him tomorrow morning, I'll let him know we can hang out sometime. Nothing big, but it would get me out of my room for a little at least."

"Wonderful. let me know when you make plans to go so we can discuss it after. I'll bring Tiana, too."

"Wait, please don't tell Tiana yet. I don't want her to freak out too much. She tends to get too involved when people she knows start dating."

"Noted," I say.

~ ~ ~

"Can you help me practice?" Duncan asks while hangs in my open campus room door.

"Yeah, of course. Let me grab my script," I tell him. We walk down to the rehearsal room – we can't use the stage because there's a performance happening in half an hour so and the theatre is filled with people.

"I practice a lot but I still get stage fright," he says. "I guess it's because I'm not really one of you."

"You are by far the most artistic future doctor I have ever met," I say.

"Which part are you nervous about? I mean we haven't even started rehearsal yet, don't be so hard on yourself," I say.

"Oh it's your first year here. It's kind of an unwritten rule that you're off-script by the beginning of rehearsal."

"Are you serious?" I ask.

"Yes. I mean Mr. Barnes won't say anything to you but I don't want him to have a preconceived notion about your work ethic when you get there. He's all about going above and beyond what you are asked to do."

"In that case I plan on keeping you here all day to help *me* practice," I say.

"As long as you promise to go to The Muse with me for a coffee after we're done."

"Deal," I say, and we begin first with the scene that we have together.

SHYLOCK
What says that fool of Hagar's offspring, ha?
JESSICA
His words were 'Farewell mistress;' nothing else.
SHYLOCK
The patch is kind enough, but a huge feeder;
Snail-slow in profit, and he sleeps by day
More than the wild-cat: drones hive not with me;
Therefore I part with him, and part with him
To one that would have him help to waste
His borrow'd purse. Well, Jessica, go in;
Perhaps I will return immediately:
Do as I bid you; shut doors after you:
Fast bind, fast find;
A proverb never stale in thrifty mind.

I finished with, JESSICA

Farewell; and if my fortune be not crost,
I have a father, you a daughter, lost.

"That was really good," he says, "now let's try it again without the script and see how far you can get."

I don't get very far. So we practice again and again and I almost forget he wants to go over his lines, and I'm not the one who went out looking to practice with him. When we are too tired to carry on we decide to get a coffee.

"I'm so glad I have someone to practice with here." I say.

"Yeah, everyone is pretty friendly and understanding that you may be having a hard time with things," he says.

"Well, most everyone. For some reason I can't put my finger on, Fleur seems to hate me."

"She can be a very jealous person."

"Why would she be jealous of me? I just got here, and she got the lead. She seemed to hate me from day one."

"Word got around that you and I met before. I know she has had a crush on me over the past few summers. We went out for a little bit but I just didn't feel the same way."

"What would that have to do with her hating me?" I ask even though I think I know the answer.

"I really like you, Olivia. But I want to take things slowly. I've gone through a lot in the past with exes and I've messed up other relationships by going too fast."

"I understand that. I really like you too. But there's someone else." I say. He looks down at the floor.

"You have a boyfriend at home?" he asks.

"Well… no." I say. He looks back up at me. "Not exactly. There's this guy, and I've had feelings for him for a long time. I don't know if I can just let that go and be with someone else right away."

"What does he have that I don't?" he asks, sounding hurt.

"We've been together our whole lives. Our Moms were friends so we grew up together. He's always been there for me, you know?"

"This guy sounds great. Why aren't you with him?"

"I was hoping I would be by now. We got kind of…close before I left. But now he's not talking to me much."

"Do any of your friends know why he's doing this? Surely he's still talking to them."

"Not that they've told me but I do plan on asking Jenna, my best friend from home, what he's been up to. I just want answers, you know?"

"Yeah. What made you like him all these years? I find it helps sometimes to dissect what you know about your relationship to see where you can go from here."

"We've known each other forever. He's always looked out for me and I feel safe around him. I've been through a lot in my life and he's been the shoulder to cry on. Boyfriends in the past haven't always been nice and he was able to see that and make sure I was always safe."

"Tell me more about that," he says.

"My high school boyfriend, Matt, was Max's best friend at the time. We started dating when we were around fourteen, we were each other's first serious relationship. Anyway, I didn't really know what a healthy relationship looked like. I just thought it was normal for him to be really possessive over me. Telling me what I should look like, say, or do. He controlled who I saw and when, and eventually started to try to isolate me from my family. It was hard because he was such a big part of my life. Just before we graduated from high school Max convinced me to break up with him. I spent many nights on his couch crying and eating pizza, and he was there for me. Eventually we started school and I met Jenna and Steven and we all became really close."

"It's good you have such a strong bond with someone like that. Why didn't it work out between the two of you? I want to know what happened and why you were being secretive before. If you feel comfortable telling me about that I'd like to know what happened."

"We hooked up before I left and he's yet to really talk to me. He responded once with a 'hi' and that's about it. I really thought this was the opportunity to be with him that I've been looking for but I guess not."

"Olivia... I know this is probably not what you want to hear right now, but I am a strong believer that everything happens for a reason. Now you know that he isn't right for you. Maybe you can consider dating someone else now that you know this is the way he is treating you. And doing that is not right of him, I'm sorry he hurt you like that."

"I guess so."

"Look at it this way, if you didn't hook up with him you would have come here and assumed that you still belonged with him. You would have gone home and maybe been in a relationship with him for some time. You would have realized you could have done better, and moved on, and probably wondered what could have happened if you weren't so hung up on him. You're an independent woman who deserves the very best, just like you are. I'm not saying that I am that person, I'm just saying that he's out there. Whoever gets to see your face the first thing in the morning will be a very lucky person."

"Thank you. Really, thank you. I knew that I deserved better than him but hearing someone else say it helped a lot. I still can't help that I have feelings for him though."

"I don't expect you to get over him right away. I just hope you're happy with whatever you choose."

"I will be." I say to reassure both him and myself.

~ ~ ~

I sit on one of the benches in the audience and wait for my turn to practice. I have a fairly minor role but we are all required to be here during all rehearsal times. I figure I would want to be here to see everyone else practice but it was pretty tiring to have to stare at Fleur up on stage with Duncan with me sitting on the sidelines.

Fleur as Portia and Cathy as Nerissa practice scene four.

PORTIA

By my troth, Nerissa, my little body is aweary of
this great world.
NERISSA
You would be, sweet madam, if your miseries were in
the Same abundance as your good fortunes are: and
yet, for aught I see, they are as sick that surfeit
with too much as they that starve with nothing. It
is no mean happiness therefore, to be seated in the
mean: superfluity comes sooner by white hairs, but
competency lives longer.

PORTIA
Good sentences and well pronounced.
NERISSA
They would be better, if well followed.
PORTIA
If to do were as easy as to know what were good to
do, chapels had been churches and poor men's
cottages princes' palaces. It is a good divine that
follows his own instructions: I can easier teach
twenty what were good to be done, than be one of the
twenty to follow mine own teaching. The brain may
devise laws for the blood, but a hot temper leaps
o'er a cold decree: such a hare is madness the
youth, to skip o'er the meshes of good counsel the
cripple. But this reasoning is not in the fashion to
choose me a husband. O me, the word 'choose!' I may
neither choose whom I would nor refuse whom I
dislike; so is the will of a living daughter curbed
by the will of a dead father. Is it not hard,
Nerissa, that I cannot choose one nor refuse none?

They finish the scene and Fleur takes a grand bow. Cathy
giggles. I hate them.

"Bravo, that was beautiful," Marcus says, clapping as he walks in.

"I have a couple of corrections to make," Mr. Barnes says. Fleur, you're great but I need more power in the voice. Cathy, I need passion. I'm getting apathy when I should be getting passion," with the word 'passion' Mary looks at Duncan and not so subtly elbows Rosie. "That a wrap for now, guys. Olivia, I would like to see you in my office so please meet me there in a couple minutes," Duncan and I exchange a glance.

"Let me know how it goes," he whispers to me. "If he does anything weird, let me know and I'll straighten him out."

I make it up to his office and waited for him outside the door.

"Please, come in." he says when he opens the door. I go in and sit down on the chair across from his desk. The walls of the room are covered in framed posters from various musicals, likely ones that he has been in or directed.

"Why did you ask to see me? I haven't really practiced too much in front of people. I mean, I've been practicing at home but not in front of you." I'm nervous to say the least. I try to stop babbling on.

"I know, and I must say I am disappointed I couldn't have given you a better part. I know how talented you are and how badly you want it. And you most certainly do have the...look we are interested in." He looks me up and down like I'm a piece of meat and he's a starving lion.

"What can I do better next year? I mean I might not be back next year but it would be good to know where I can improve anyway." I want to go along with what he was saying so he will let me leave his office.

"It's all about who you know. I'm going to give you my personal cell phone number and I want you to call me if you ever need anything."

"Thank you," I take the number. When I leave I almost run up to Duncan's room. This is the first time I have been in there and as soon as he open the door I am in a sea of blue. The Chelsea Football Club crest is plastered on every part of the wall on his side of the room, and some of it was flooding on to James' side of the room. There are pictures of what has to be Duncan in the very early years of his soccer practice.

"How'd it go?" He asks when he opens the door.

"He said something about wanting to see me more often and maybe we can set up an arrangement."

"We need to go to someone about him, what he's doing isn't right. I mean if she's paying him then that's unethical, and I would have to look into it but I think what he is saying to you is sexual harassment. He can't do that."

"I know but I don't want to mess up what I have going here. The other staff members like me a lot. If I report him, what if they think I'm lying and either kick me out of the part I have or don't invite me back again?"

"That's true. It's hard though because I know what he's doing is wrong."

"Just leave it for now. We won't do anything too drastic just yet. Just let me think about it."

Chapter Ten

Love is a smoke made with a fume of sighs - Romeo and Juliet, William Shakespeare

"How'd it go?" I ask Harper about her date with Kenneth. We're going for a walk around Regent Park with Tiana. I made it my personal mission at the beginning of the summer to go to as many public parks as possible. Even with the little bit of running I've been doing, I've been slowly seeing a muffin top appear at the top of the waistband of my shorts. When I realized this, I made plans to get out and do some more walking, especially during the few days we've been getting perfect weather. I relish the few times I'm able to go for a run in a warm, well lit park, but those times are few. We're surrounded by dark green foliage that is newly dampened by last night's rainfall. The summer heat has warmed the air, so we're all in dresses and sandals that make our feet and ankles wet with dew.

"How'd what go?" Tiana asks and sits down on a bench.

"Harper went on a date," I say.

"Harper went on a date?"

"Yes. I did. Can stop now so I can tell you about it?" Harper says. I clear my notebooks off the bed and pat it, motioning her to sit down next to me.

"First went went out to a movie. You know that little cinema close by? A really cute place. Anyway, he took me there and we went out for dinner after."

"You have to tell us more than that," Tiana says, "are you seeing him again?"

"Yes. We're going out on Friday, actually."

"What did you talk about?" Tiana asks.

"He told me a little bit about his family and where he's from. We grew up pretty close by each other, actually. He's really cool. I'm not going to say that we're going to be official or anything but I liked spending time with him and I'm excited to see him again." With that, Tiana begins flicking through her Instagram photos to get ideas of outfits to fit Harper that she would consider wearing on the date. Tiana runs a fashion blog and chronicles her daily outfits online. The suggestions aren't much use, since Tiana wears mostly high heels, which

Harper wrinkles her nose when Tiana has the very though of suggesting them.

~ ~ ~

"I. Am. So. Ready. For. Today." Tiana says as soon as she opens her eyes. She gets the quickest shower I can remember her doing since we've been here. I try to remember what is so special about today.

"Like, this is always the best day of the summer. I can finally put all my expertise – and believe me, there's a lot of it – to good use. God bless the costuming department for knowing about this flawless costume shop that actually isn't too far from here." Ah, right. It's the day we are going to pick out our costumes for the production. When I first got here I assumed that they keep costumes for each play in some storage room ready to go. They do have some, but they also want to know how much we know about our characters and the time period we're working in. This means that Tiana will be working in her nirvana for the next couple weeks. She's one of few fashion design majors here and the only one with such a strong interest in historical fashion so she's the one to go to for the fashion advice and the one who will be instructing us on how to do our hair and makeup. She is particularly excited to dress me. I decide I need to hit the pavement and go for a run before we leave so I grab a quick breakfast of an apple and half a bagel with peanut butter and head out.

The Thames at sunrise is so beautiful. There are a couple of other runners and people walking dogs. There're a small white one that takes a particular fondness to me. It probably thinks I will be much nicer to it that it's owner, who insists on using (hopefully) animal safe purple dye on it's ears and big, yellow bows on the ears and collar. Sorry pooch, I don't think I'll be allowed to take you back to campus. I'm getting out of shape since I've been neglecting my running while I am here, so I push harder to try to get back some of the progress I've lost. I know I've been gaining weight since I've been here. Not too much, or even an amount some people would notice. But I've noticed. My jeans fit on my hips a little more snugly. I haven't had another purging relapse since that time in the tube station, though I've had urges. I can resist almost all of them, except when they have to do with Michael. When I was in recovery from the eating disorder though, I found running helped. I wasn't allowed to run in the treatment centre. I was still too fragile for that. I started running only two years ago, when I first got to university. It was a slow start. It started with me huffing and puffing on the indoor track for about five minutes every other day, and eventually I extended that a little longer each time. Before I really knew how much better I was getting, I was running five kilometres on a daily basis. Now my standard is eight kilometres, three days each week, and a longer run on the weekends. I still haven't gathered up the courage to sign up for a race, or even a running club. I don't like running with other people. I don't want to run on a treadmill where I'll be comparing myself to the person next to me. I want to run on a trail or even the sidewalk, where I can pass right by people. Running is my time to have an excuse to be my introverted self and listen to my favourite audiobooks while strengthening my body. I've learned to love the feeling of my strong thighs and my heart helping me push my body forward. I was so close to losing the ability to do something like that. When I run I feel as if I can protect myself and I'll never be in a situation that I can't run away from. I don't want to be helpless ever again.

    I finish my five kilometres in a pretty good time. I know for my sanity I need to remember to make time for running a couple of times a week while I'm here. After I get back to my room and and get a shower, I have just enough time to hop on the bus where I sit next to Tiana.

    "I know you're not huge on the fluffy dresses, but Harper is even less into it. And dressing the boys is not nearly as fun." Tiana spends the bus ride chattering our ears off about the kinds of things she wanted to pick up. Apparently the Globe has a contract with a local costume shop so they can borrow things as they please for a pretty low rate. It is not a lower rate, though, if you damage or lose one of the pieces. I've heard the dresses can cost upwards of £10 000 each, and we're responsible for each of our own costumes while we're using them.

    The bus parks next to a building that looks like an old church. It has stained-glass windows and was made of red brick; the lawn was even covered in Celtic crosses to look like a cemetery. I wonder if it is a church that was renovated into a shop and if the graves were actually real. The hair on my arms starts to stand up and I try not to think about the graves, just in case they are. When we walk in we are greeted by a young woman who claims she and her Mother own the store and that we are to feel free to ask her if we need anything or have any questions.

Tiana takes my hand and leads me to the back of the store and we begin shuffling through the racks of clothing.

"This. Try this one." She presses a gold ball gown to my chest. I'm not sure it would look good on me but I decide it isn't worth the argument.

I get into the dressing room and take off my clothes. I kind of regret doing that, because now I can't open the door and ask for Tiana's help getting it on. I awkwardly open the corset back and gingerly step in to the bodice of the dress and wiggle it up to my chest. I hold the top of the dress and try to at least use the clips that are in the dressing room to clip the back of the dress so it doesn't fall off me. There isn't a mirror on the inside of the dressing room, which is a total pet peeve of mine. Don't people realize that an evil French bitch from hell is also costume shopping with me, and I can't let her see me in anything less than perfect? Also, knowing Tiana , she probably has her phone out to snap a picture of me for Instagram while she's waiting. Regardless, I know she won't let me forget it if I don't show her myself in all her choices, so I step out of the dressing room.

I look like a cake topper.

"I love it," she says when I walk out.

"You've got to be kidding me," I say and motion toward the big mirror. I see Fleur in a slinky black number a couple feet away from me, taking a picture of herself on her phone with her lips in a pouty expression and a pose that makes her look like she has the body of a fitness model. Cathy looks at me and laughs before taking a picture with Rosie, each giving kissy mouths and peace signs.

"No, its great. Your waist looks tiny."

"I do not care about how small my waist looks. I can't breathe and I'm going to trip over this train." The fabric trails two feet behind me. "I'm not wearing this."

"So? Everyone is trying on things that they won't wear. Its part of the fun. You really think Her Majesty is going to wear *that*?" She nods at Fleur, who is still photographing herself. Good God, how many pictures does she need? I hear Tiana utter what sounds like 'slut' under her breath. "Fine. Try this one," she says and hands me a dress that looks about the same but in bright red.

"This is way too bright. I'm not a lead, I can't wear a giant red dress if I'm not a main character."

"You're right. Try this." She hands me an indigo blue gown with silver embroidered detailing and a scoop neck. This is better.

I put it on and the sleeves fall over my shoulders instead of on top of them but I think that is how it was supposed to be.

"That. Is. Amazing," she says when I come out. "Try these." She hands me a silver glittery hair clip to keep my bangs out of my face and a pair of big, sparkly, matching clip on earrings. This, I can get used to. When I'm done Duncan and James come over.

"You look great," James says.

"Stunning," Duncan adds, and looks me down from head to toe.

"Great. I'll go tell the lady which style number you want. I can't wait to do your hair and makeup and see it with the dress, you are so going to outshine you-know-who." Tiana leaves us there.

"Just let me get changed and we'll go find you guys something," I say to the boys. When I come back out Duncan and James are in the tuxedo section of the store. Everything is pretty straightforward for them. Most of the men's stuff looks pretty much the same. When we are done there I take a look around the other racks and saw all the different things they have. They have rich ball gowns, suits, things are well made but look like they are nearly falling apart which are for peasant characters. They even have things for people to dress up as animals like donkeys and lions.

Tiana and I return to our campus room and she is on the top of the world.

"We don't have classes for the rest of the day and I'm bursting with ideas. Sit down." She nods towards me and then the area of the bathroom she dubbed her makeshift vanity. I sit down.

"Teach me everything you know," I say.

"Impossible. But I do want to brainstorm makeup looks on you." She begins with covering some of my freckles and acne spots. "I love how pale your skin is. It means I don't have to go crazy with the white powder. It was all the fashion at the time to be pale. Apparently only peasants had tanned skin." She laughs and looks down at her own dark skin. "I would not have put up with that racist crap, and I still don't, but I have to stay true to what was right for the time period." She moves onto my cheeks and makes them a flush bright pink colour. She covers my eyelids in a light brown shade and she reaches into her makeup bag and pulls out a pair of false eyelashes.

"I think we can stop here," I say.

"Okay, please don't tell me you've never worn a pair of false lashes before."

"I have no interest in gluing fake hair onto my eyes."

"You'll need to do it for the performance. They always make people wear them. And they're not on your eyes, they're on your eyelashes."

"The skin connecting to my eyes, you mean. Besides, maybe we should wait until then so I can surprised everyone with the amount of fabulous I will be. I wouldn't want to spoil the surprise on you know."

"I know you're just saying that to get out of wearing them, but you're right." I look in the mirror because she's done now. I do look good, though abnormally pale. Without the white powder I could see myself doing this every day.

I wash off the makeup and sit down at the little table in our room. Tiana decided we're going to have a full pamper day so she gathers her mani pedi equipment and starts filling a bowl with warm soapy water. She brings it over and puts my hands in the water to soak.

"Tiana ... I want to talk to you about something," I say.

"Of course. Anything."

"I saw Mr. Barnes a couple times to practice, and once he called me into his office. Anyway, he was being super creepy. Duncan says it could be considered sexual harassment."

"I know a little bit about sexual harassment..." I hear Tiana's breath tighten as she tell me. "just for... personal reasons. Anyway, you need to do something about him. What he's doing isn't right." She starts pushing back the cuticle of my short, bitten nails.

"I normally don't tell people this, but there's a reason I know a lot about sexual harassment and stuff. My family doesn't like to talk about it. But my Dad is in prison right now because of something similar."

"What? Did he hurt someone?" I ask.

"It began with small comments to a woman at his work. Then it continued. First she told him to stop and then he wouldn't. She went to his boss and he laughed it off. A lot of people don't know how corrupt the military can be. These guys are supposed to protect us. I mean most of them are great guys, but some of the aren't. Dad kept harassing her and then she ended up in the hospital. He had...assaulted her. Raped her, I mean. When she went to the police and told them about the situation they agreed to help her but most people expected her to have done something sooner. They expected her to prevent her own attack. Dad kept saying that if she had behaved herself he wouldn't have had to do it. He also said that she was drunk and he didn't realize it was so bad. This all happened when I was pretty young so I don't remember too much but I searched for it online and read some of the news articles. He's been in prison ever since he was convicted. I was actually raised by my aunt and uncle because Mom had some issues with dealing with it all. She drank a lot." Tiana finishes filing my nails, and won't meet my gaze. Her eyes focus on drying my hands with a plush white towel.

"I don't know what to say." I say after we sit in silence for a moment.

"I know. It's hard for me to tell people and even harder for them to understand. I just want you to be safe," she says.

"I promise I will go to someone soon and tell them about what is happening. Until then, we'll figure out what he's doing with Fleur too."

"First thing's first, though… pink nail polish," Tiana says and starts shaking the bottle.

Armed with matching glittery pink polish on our nails, we decide to go to Mrs. Rogers, the costuming professor. Our conversation gives us a boost of confidence so we want to go today We're lucky this is during her office hours so we quickly make our way over. We knock on the half open door.

"Yes, ladies, come in," she says and gestures to the chairs across from her desk. I look around the room, the walls are covered in feather boas and there are dress form mannequins draped in fabric and measuring tapes.

"What can I help you two with? I'm sure my favourite student isn't having troubles in my class." She smiles warmly at Tiana, and she feigns embarrassment.

"Actually, we're here because of Olivia," Tiana says. They both look at me.

"Well, Mr. Barnes has been making me feel uncomfortable lately. He says really creepy things sometimes, and I heard a conversation with him and Fleur and I think she's paying him or sleeping with him to get her further in her career and that's really wrong and he can't do that and I don't know who else to go to." I stop and take a deep breath. I'm trying not to cry and I can tell Mrs. Rogers is a little horrified by my stream of consciousness I just made her experience.

"So... you're saying that he has been acting inappropriately with his students?"

"Yes, I am."

"That's a very serious accusation."

"I know. I wouldn't have said anything if it wasn't a big deal to me. I don't feel comfortable with him around. And I don't exactly know what is going on with Fleur but I know it's unethical." I say. I am gaining my confidence back. I know going to someone about him is the right thing.

"If this is something you say you're experiencing I'm sure there is something going on here. I would like you to write down all the details you can remember, including dates and times. I'm going to take it to the Human Resources department and I'm sure they'll know where to go from there. We'll also have to talk about Fleur, you know."

"I know. I just would like it if you didn't mention that it was us who came to you. I know she already doesn't like me and I don't want to make it worse."

"Of course, this will just be between the three of us until someone higher up decides what to do about it." She hands me a pen and paper and I begin writing a statement. I'm not sure if this is what would normally happens in such a situation but neither of us have been through this before so we don't know what to do. I finish the letter, sign and date it, and give it to her.

"Great, thanks. I'll take this down now. I'm sure you can expect a phone call soon from someone from HR. Try to attend your classes and act like everything is normal. Please don't let this ruin your summer, you're a great student and I know you've been having a good time up until this point. You're a strong girl and you can handle this." She gives me a big hug. I'm glad there is someone here who will look out for me.

Tiana and I go to lunch and then to our afternoon classes like Mrs. Rogers said we should. I have to go to my theatre class, and she to her advanced costuming class. I go to Harper"s room before class so we can walk down together and I can fill her in on what happened.

"So you really think they're going to do something about this? I mean what he did was totally wrong but there is no evidence against him and he is really well loved in the theatre world. They could favour him."

"I know and I've considered that. But I have to do what's right. If he did this to me, what's to say he won't do it again to someone else, or even do something worse to someone, like assault them? I can't let that happen."

"That's true. I'm sure you're doing the right thing and so will they."

I go in to my class, hoping I will be able to focus a little bit and about twenty minutes in, someone knocks on the door.

"Hello, I'm looking for a Fleur LeClerc," she says when the teacher opens the door. Fleur stands up and tries to walk over. "Take your books," she says, "you won't be back to finish class."

Chapter Eleven

This above all: to thine own self be true - Hamlet, William Shakespeare

"HR wants to speak to you," Mrs. Rogers says when she knocks on my door that Saturday morning.

"I thought they would," I say.

"Come with me. You'll be okay."

I walk with her down to the Globe, in a back room with some offices in it. A lady sits at one of the desks. It is just her and I in the room. Mrs. Rogers is only sent to go get me but she isn't to be there when I am being questioned.

"Hello, Olivia. My name is Cassie Anderson and I'm head of the Human Resources department here. I normally don't deal with claims such as your own but we haven't had too any of this nature so it's an uncommon thing for me to deal with. I'll have you know that this is a very serious accusation and Mr. Barnes is a very loved man here. If this is a false claim I would have to ask you to leave and you would lose your role in the final performance, and he could choose to press charges." So this is the woman that had the email exchange with Fleur that we found in her file. She didn't seem to do much to prevent this from happening with her students. I'm taken aback by her abruptness. I was expecting her to treat the topic with a little more sensitivity.

"This isn't a false claim. Everything that I said in my letter is true," I say with an air of confidence.

"I've already spoken to Fleur and she said that what you said wasn't true, and that you've been targeting her since the roles were announced. She has been here for years. I know her father and he is a very trustworthy man who raised a trustworthy daughter. I highly doubt she would lie to me."

"How much exactly do you know about her? I'm good friends with someone she confided in in the past... I won't tell you everything I've been told because it's not my place, her father doesn't support her wanting to have a career in the arts. If her father doesn't financially support her being here, how do you think she pays the high program fees? She can't possibly work to support herself and pay for this. But there are ways for young women to get money for minimal work if they are willing to do it," I say.

Mrs. Anderson's eyes looks like they are going to pop out of her head. "What are you saying, here, exactly?"

"I think you know what I mean."

"Well... you seem very sure of your claim. I haven't spoken to Mr. Barnes yet, but I would like to speak to Fleur again. I have her outside." She gets up and opens the door to let her in. Fleur sits down next to me, wordless.

"You both know why you're here." Mrs. Anderson says, "and one of you is lying. Please, tell me who it is."

"She is," we say in unison and proceeded to glare at each other.

"Alright girls, I'm going to leave the room. I want you to discuss what happened and agree on something to tell me. Open the door when you're done and we can take it from there." She gets up and leaves. Fleur sits there with her arms crossed, staring at the wall and refusing to acknowledge me.

~ ~ ~

Tiana and I talk a little bit longer and decide that we needed to do something fun to get our minds off what was going on so we decide to see the performance of *A Midsummer Night's Dream* that night.

"I love the costumes they use for this one," she says, "often times they'll reuse the same costumes for multiple plays, but most of these ones are unique. I've seen them do this play a couple times before. You'll love the Pyramus and Thisbe scene. It's *hilarious*." We hear the music to indicate the beginning of the performance and stop talking. My favourite scene has always the one of the four lovers in the forest, and this performance does it so well.

Seeing these professionals on the stage makes me remember why I'm here. I didn't come here to be a victim of some sick man. I'm here to create the art of performance. I want every single person in this city to line up just to see me perform on stage some day. And it will happen. I just need to work harder and keep my chin up. These professionals started where I am now, and I will not let them down. I won't leave early and let my family down. Most importantly, I'll make the most out of this opportunity and not let myself down.

After the performance we go out to The Crown for a pint. The pub is filled with students, as usual. We see Harper and Duncan playing darts in the corner and James is sitting down at the table next to him. Fleur is hanging around Duncan. Tiana and I share a glance and walk over.
"Hey, guys," James says. "How was it?"
"So good," I say, "I swear if I didn't have to study I would be in there every night."
"I don't blame you," Harper says, "you should see their performance of Romeo and Juliet. I know it's the stereotypical favourite, but there's a reason it's seen as so good."
"You're crazy," I reply, "way too over-hyped."
"Them is fightin' words," James says in an exaggerated Southern drawl, and we all laugh.
They continue debating about the different plays they've seen but I'm watching Fleur out of the corner of my eye. She has a hand on Duncan's waist and he's leaning against the wall. Here I am in just a pair of jeans and a sweatshirt. She's dressed up in a black sparkly dress

that shows off her legs and cleavage with hair and make-up done. She looks ready to walk the runway. I sit in the corner with my pint of cider and take out my script, going over my lines.

"Why so quiet?" James comes over and sits down next to me as he asks me.

"I'm okay… just kind of homesick, you know?" I reply.

"I know. I have a lot of fun here every summer but it's hard to be away from home."

"Tell me about yourself. I don't know much about you besides you are from Virginia Beach and you're dating Tiana ."

"Well, I was actually born here in England. My Dad still lives here. My parents were never married. Mom got pregnant while she was here for a vacation once and she took me back to the US to raise me. Dad visits me every Christmas and I come here in the summers. We have a pretty good relationship considering that we never actually lived together. He's a pretty good guy."

"What do your parents do?"

"Mom's a writer and Dad's a mechanic. Nothing too glamorous but they're great. Mom writes mainly plays so she raised me in the theatre."

"Seems to be that way with most people here."

"Yeah, Shakespeare is kind of niche as far as beginning actors are concerned. It's a competitive program and a lot of people either find the material too hard or intimidating, or they're just not interested in it. They're even taking Shakespeare out of some classrooms because the kids dislike it so much."

"That's awful."

"I agree. I plan on making it kind of fun." His eyes glow in excitement. "I've been writing some screenplays with my Mom. Like taking some of Shakespeare's original plays and putting a modern spin on it, hoping people would realize that the issues he deals with are timeless and universal. So far nothing we've written like that is being produced but who knows, maybe one day."

"I think that would be a fabulous idea. I would be the first to audition for one of the roles," I say.

"You would be the first I would hire."

I hear Fleur giggle and see her touch Duncan's bicep.

"I really don't like them together," James says quietly to me.

"Can we go for a walk?" I ask.

"Of course." We got up and left the building and began walking down the road.

"I can tell you really like him," he says.

"I do."

"Have you told him that?"

"No. I don't know how to bring it up."

"You need to. I know Fleur has been after him for a while, and he's not crazy about her, but maybe she'll try to convince him there is something good about her. If he doesn't know how you feel he might get close to her, and you'll be upset."

"I know. I will find a way to tell him soon," I say.

"Has he told you much about his past relationships?"

"I know he dated Harper for a bit, if that's what you mean."

"Not exactly. Look, I know you haven't known him for very long so I'm not surprised he hasn't told you what happened yet. Just know that he's not really in the place to be dating anyone right now."

"That's easy for you to say." I say, "you aren't the one he's been flirting with, and the one with the boy at home she needs to get over, and the one who thinks he's a really great guy." I can't believe I am telling all this to a guy I hardly know, but what could it hurt? He's Duncan's best friend and there is a chance Tiana told him everything already.

"I know what happened with the guy at home… Max, is it?" Apparently my suspicions were right about Tiana being a big mouth.

"Yeah, that's him."

"He's no good for you. You're a great girl. And I'm sure you and Duncan would be really happy together but he's my boy, I need to look out for what's best with him. He's dealt with heartbreak before and a long distance relationship isn't best for him. It's hard for most people."

"I know. I've never had to do that kind of a relationship before so I wouldn't even know what to do. But if two people were in love, it could really work… right?"

"Maybe. I know you like Duncan, but I also know that you're not over Max. He seems like an awful guy though so I don't get why you still like him."

"I, just… I've been through a lot with him. I don't want to talk about it. But I owe him a lot."

"You owe yourself a healthy relationship. I don't think you can get it from Duncan or Max. You need to take care of yourself."

"But you don't know how hard it is to let go."

Chapter Twelve

The fool doth think he is wise, but the wise man knows himself to be a fool - As You Like It, William Shakespeare

"Did you pick up the cake?" I ask Tiana.

"It's in the fridge in the cafeteria. I couldn't put it in the student kitchen because I was afraid he would see it," she says. It's been so hot out lately I'm afraid the icing will melt if we leave it out at room temperature. Luckily, the chef at the campus restaurant loves us so we don't have to worry about not having a place to put Duncan's birthday cake.

I ordered the cake last week. I made sure it was vanilla with lots of blue food colouring.

Tiana and I decorate the lounge with blue and white streamers and a big "Happy Birthday Duncan" sign on the wall. There are a couple of traditions for birthdays over the summer. First thing Duncan will notice in the morning is that James decorated his door. Normally this consists of a couple of streamers on the outside of the door. This year, we decide Duncan will wake up to a balloon avalanche. Duncan is infamous for his morning grogginess so this struck us as the most hilarious idea. We blew up balloons and manage to use streamers to trap them to the door. The door opens from the inside so he will be flooded with balloons when he opens the door.

We excitedly wait in the hallway outside Duncan's door.

James texts us from inside the room:

He's brushing his teeth. He'll be out soon.

I hope James can keep a straight face so that Duncan won't realize we're up to something.

We see the doorknob turn and wait. Duncan swings it open and the balloons wash over him, stunning him for a moment before he realizes what happened.

"What the blood hell?!" He asks and flings one of the small balloons out of his face.

"HAPPY BIRTHDAY!" Tiana, Harper, James, and I yell in unison.

"Ya bunch a wankers," Duncan says, laughing, "how did you manage that?"

"I wrangled the balloons together by my self out of sheer will and determination," James says, taking credit for all of our work. Tiana playfully glares at him and stick out her tongue.

After breakfast we tell everyone to meet us in the lounge for drinks and cake, Duncan's friends have pitched in so we got a couple cases of beer and cider and a few bottles of wine. I think my favourite part about this country is the cheap booze. Maybe I like the men the best. No, definitely the cheap wine. We're going to spend all day celebrating, and we're ready for it. After we polish off what we bought, which is never enough for how many people show up when they hear the word *party*, we continue down at The Crown and everyone starts swapping stories about their lives back home and of things that happened in summers in the past at the Globe.

"Remember that one time James forgot all his lines for a scene and just improved it?" Harper asks everyone.

"Yes, he was Benvolio that year," Tiana says.

"Good thing he didn't get Romeo like he had wanted or he would have shut the whole production down," Duncan adds.

"Hey now, I was the best part of that *damn* show. You were all boring. I made that stuffy performance bearable," he slurs, and shoves his pointed index finger in the air in front of his face to emphasize his point.

"That's not what the reviews said. We're lucky anyone won the contract with you messing everything up," Tiana laughs. We carry on through the night, just having a good time and enjoying ourselves until we get tired and decide to walk home.

"I have a little gift for you," I say as I pull Duncan aside.

"You helped plan this whole night, I couldn't ask for anything more," he says.

"No, I really want to. I want you to go out with me tomorrow tonight." I hand him a handmade card. I drew him wearing a Chelsea shirt and holding a soccer ball. He opens it up and sees the two tickets for the museum and a game at Chelsea stadium. Tickets normally sell out pretty quickly so I was lucky to have gotten them.

"I know you're a big Chelsea fan and I could help but want to go see what they're all about since you like them so much."

"Nothing would make me happier than bringing you to a match."

"Wonderful. I'm looking forward to it." I smile. "We leave tomorrow so I hope you're ready. You got to surprise me with a spontaneous first date, now I get to take you on the second."

"So the Eye was a date?" He asks playfully.

"Yes. At the time I didn't think it was, but I have since changed my mind."

"Sounds fair to me. Goodnight, Olivia. I'll see you bright and early in the morning," he says before going in to his room.

~ ~ ~

The next morning I have an unexpected visit from Fleur.

"I'll never tell you what exactly happened with Mr. Barnes, but it isn't happening any more. I hope you're happy," she says.

"Well, I can't say anything about the situation makes me happy," I say.

"What did you want me to do?"

"I wanted you to do what's right."

"Well okay then. Whatever you say."

"Fleur... why do you hate me so much?"

"You came in here like you owned the fucking place. I can't believe you scholarship kids think you can come in here in the place that I worked to hard to get to, you get everything I had to kill to earn like it's nothing."

"What are you talking about? You got the lead. I got a minor role," I say.

"It's not just the acting. You took my spot as Tiana's best friend. You managed to have Duncan wrapped around your stupid little finger. Just because he met you by accident before you got here, he think you're some gift from God. He's in love with you and you don't even care. You'll probably end up with the contract, just because you couldn't leave well enough alone. I can't believe I just told you all this." Fleur finally takes a breath. We are still standing outside my door. I open it.

"Come in so we can talk. Tiana's gone so we'll have some privacy." I say.

"No."

"Come on."

"I don't want to."

"You need to. Talking about it will help."

"Fine." She walks in and sat down at the chair by the window. I sit at the one across from her. I kind of felt like a therapist.

"Now, tell me about you and Duncan," I say.

"Promise you won't tell anyone what we say here?"

"Promise," I say.

"Okay. I guess if you ask him he'll tell you anyway, so might as well tell you my side of it all first. We got here for the first time on the same year. We were both freshmen in college. We actually met up at the airport before we got to the Globe. We were both in line at the information kiosk when I asked for directions on how to get there. He was behind me and suggested we walk together. I agreed."

"Oh my god, does he wait around Heathrow scoping out girls to hit on?" I ask jokingly. Fleur laughs.

"Apparently so. But anyway, we got close that summer. Tiana and I were roommates, she started dating James. The four of us spent all our time together so it was expected for us to get close. I got a pretty big crush on him and I thought he liked me too, but apparently not. I tried to hook up with him a couple times. He said he doesn't have sex outside of a relationship but I don't see that being true. He's so hot, why would he do that?" She looks genuinely unsure of why he wouldn't want to sleep with her, "anyway I figured he wasn't interested after that."

"Just because he's hot doesn't mean he's going to go around fucking people. But I guess that was good of him though, not to hook up with you and then pretend you don't exist."

"I doubt that would be an improvement. At least then I could seduce him or even have him for a little bit. Maybe then he would want to stay," Fleur says.

"No, it's not better. That was me a couple weeks ago." I explain what had happened, or not happened, between Max and I.

"I'm sorry. I really am. You deserve better than that. I mean, I still think you're bitch, but no girl deserves that," she says.

"Me too. I'm sorry, I mean," I say, trying to ignore the sting her words always manage to leave.

"I'm still pissed about you going and telling on me about Mr. Barnes. You know that, right?"

"Yeah. Also, what exactly happened between you two? I've guessed but I still don't know for sure."

"I have had to do this for a while now. My parents won't pay to support me while I'm working in the arts. Papa's a shareholder here, he owns part of the Globe but he has no respect for the arts. He thinks this whole thing is stupid. But he's never actually seen a play here himself. So I've needed to make the money in other ways."

"How, exactly?"

"Honestly, call it what you will, but I have sex for money and connections."

"You're an... escort?"

"Yes. I'm not ashamed of it, but what I do isn't exactly respectable so I don't want it to get out. I also want to be known for my talent on the stage, not my talent in bed," she says.

"I guess so. But do you really want to be doing this?"

"No but what choice do I have? I have to make it somehow."

"But how? Aren't you afraid? And like… ew," I say, not trying to hide the look of disgust on my face.

"More people are doing it than you realize. I just get paid for what you sluts give out for free. Look, I need to go. But can you please tell me again you won't tell anyone? I mean if you do I'll just deny it but still. Please."

"I won't. I promise. But Fleur, why are you telling me all of this? You could have just kept denying it."

"As much as you annoy me, I think what Barnes did to you is shitty. I won't support someone trying to fuck someone against their will, you know? You have my support in going after him. But if you tell anyone that, I'll kill you."

Chapter Thirteen

All things are ready, if our mind be so -
Henry V, William Shakespeare

    I know nothing about professional soccer. I played soccer for about two months in elementary school, so I know the basics of the game, but I've never even watched a professional match on TV, and here I am about to watch England's most well-loved sport in their best city. With the best guy I've ever met.

    "I've been here before, of course," he says after I ask about why likes soccer so much. "My Dad is a big fan so he passed it down to me. We used to go to a match together every year before he got too busy from work to spend too much time away from the house. After they got busy with work I mostly just hung out with Darcy."

"Darcy?"

"My sister. She's two years younger than me. We're really close."

"That's nice. My brother and I aren't that close. We're pretty far apart in age so I would guess that's why."

"That's too bad but it does make sense. Now, do you want a crash course on football?" He smiles at me.

"Yes," We get in the line for the museum. The building is all blue and white and emblazoned with the Chelsea crest. It's slightly rainy but Duncan's mood can't be brought down no matter what the weather. He knows he's surrounded by people who love sports as much as he does.

"So what other sports do you watch?" I ask.
"I watch every sport."
"You can't watch all of them."
"I do."
"Even golf?"
"Even golf."
"Tennis?"
"Yes."
"Basketball"
"Of course."
"Hmm…Cricket?"

"Yes."

"Synchronized swimming?"

"That's not a sport."

"Why not?"

"That isn't a sport."

"Why not? It's athletic."

"It doesn't have a quantitative winner. There is no ball going in to a net, it's just a matter of opinion who wins. Sure, there are some variables in sports and people can debate if a player was off-side like basketball or tennis, but at the end of the day, if you don't get the ball in the net, you don't get the point for it. Swimming, figure skating, things like that are more like…arts. They're great arts, and they take years of hard work and practice but they are not sports. Sports have data."

"But why so many sports? Why do you like them so much?"

"It's amazing to see the players develop. They grow over the years. There are some players on the teams I watch and love now that were just starting their career when I was a kid. I saw them appear on the scene, sign for one of my favourite teams, and a lot of those guys are retiring from their athletic careers. I probably started loving sports, especially soccer, at a good time. My favourite team was doing well, but seeing a group of people you love do something amazing never gets old. You root for them and when they win, you win, too. It's a community I'll always have. Even if you see someone walking down the road and you're in a city where you don't know anybody, sometimes you'll see someone wearing your team crest and it's like, an instant best friend. You can talk with that person for hours now just because of that one thing. Maybe that leads to a deeper conversation and a stronger bond you wouldn't have had if they weren't wearing that. That's why I wear my colours every day."

I think about what he said as we move through a display of shirts and other sports related merchandise. I don't think I've ever thought my passions through that throughly, and I wish I felt that strongly about something. Duncan whispers in my ear everything the tour guide was saying.

"And this is the shirt that Drogba wore, when we won against Manchester City" The tour guide says.

"Actually..." Duncan begins correcting the guide. I have to hold in both giggles and extreme embarrassment. We both come out on the other end laughing.

"So now I know that if I need to learn something about sports, you should be the first one I go to." I say.

"Well, I would hope so. I can be your personal expert on that, thank you very much."

"I would expect no less." Soon it's time for the game to start so we find our seats.

"I wish I could stand up here, but we're not allowed. I can never sit while watching a match at home."

"Why aren't you allowed to stand?"

"Oh, you know... riots and stuff."

"You say that too casually. I want to get in to sports, but forgive me if I won't get *that* in to it," I say with raised eyebrows.

"It's hard not to," he says, "I may have even been known to take my shirt off during particularly exciting matches, though it has only happened once or twice."

"I'll also try to refrain from getting *that* excited."

"Well that's too bad for me," he laughs.

The match begins and we are consumed in the world of sports.

The match is Chelsea against Queens Park Rangers. I don't expect to be able to understand what is happening but the sports announcer is able to name the players and tell everyone what is happening. I know Duncan could have explained it to me but I didn't want to talk to him while he was watching the match, I knew he was enjoying it. It didn't take long before I know Duncan is a fan of the right team.

"And here we have Chelsea coming up strong," he says in a thick English accent.

"Sturridge beginning to take the shot... and he scores! First of the match!" Duncan cheers, I clap loudly. I can tell he wants to jump up but but restrains himself.

"Next is Terry, let's see if he can keep Chelsea in the lead here. He does it! We end up with a six to one win. Duncan was and I are both elated.

"That was really cool," I say once it's over.

"You really liked it?" He asks.

"I would watch it again," I say.

I can tell that Duncan is almost high from the excitement of the match. (He insists I call it a match, and football, not soccer.) I know nothing about football so this is an eye-opening experience for me. He's in his nirvana. I'm glad to see him enjoy this so much because he sees me in my haven at the Globe every day.

"I'm starving. Are you hungry?"

"I could eat," I say.

We go out for burgers and he talks about the match.

"I mean, it was flawless," he says. "I can't believe you did this for me, this is amazing. And we even won."

"Of course I would do this for you. And hey, you're doing me a favour. I said I wanted to do everything I could while I was here and you managed to help me with that."

"Any time," he smiles, "so what brought you here in the first place?"

"You," I laugh.

"No, not to the match. To London. I know you got a scholarship but I wasn't sure why you applied to the program."

"Well, my teacher thought it would be a good experience. I almost didn't go but then I got a scholarship and was able to come."

"Why did you choose this program? You could have gotten into any summer program you wanted."

"I love Shakespeare, and not just because it's romantic or the stereotypical thing to like as an English major. I actually have dyslexia," I say. "I couldn't read well for most of my life. I struggled through everything in school. Spelling tests were always the worst. Anyway, I was told I couldn't handle the regular classes anymore once we got to ninth grade. They wanted me to take the more basic classes. I knew I couldn't get into a University with that diploma so I knew I needed to work harder and get into the regular class. They said I couldn't get in to the class until I could handle the circular, but said I could replace the required play, *Julius Caesar*, with something else. I chose *A Midsummer Night's Dream* because I thought it would be funny. It was. I really enjoyed it and have felt very connected to his work ever since. I mean, the stuff is great. He was very original and outspoken in a time that was very censored which I admire."

"How were you able to read it?" He asks.

"With help. Max read it out loud to me. He put on the English accent, and acted out the play with action figures as the characters and everything."

"That's wonderful. I'm so glad you chose to come here."

"Me too."

"Another thing, if you don't mind me asking. What is the deal with you and Max lately?"

"Nothing has been going on with us, though I would like to be with him when I get home if I could. He has helped me through a lot in the past. I know I need to let it go, but it's hard, I guess. That's all."

"I understand," he says.

"I really like you," I blurt out.

"I like you too."

"But do you ever think we could be...together?"

"Long distance would be really hard."

"I know."

"So we're not going to try and make it work?"

"I didn't say that."

"Okay."

"What if you go home and hang out with Max again?"

"If we're together you know you can trust me."

"I know."

"Also there's something about your past that you're not telling me."

"What makes you think that?" He asks.

"James told me you're not telling me everything."

"But I told you about Harper ."

"I know. Someone who isn't Harper ."

"Damnit, James," he mutters under his breath.

"It's not that big of a deal," he says, "It's just hard for me to talk about. I'll tell you later, I promise."

"Okay. So just so we all know where we stand. We're just friends for now, and you're going to tell me what's going on with you when you're ready?"

"Yes."

"Okay."

"In that case, I'm ordering pie and we're going to have a conversation that isn't filled with serious topic matter."

"Sounds like a plan to me."

We decide not to go straight home from the restaurant. We take the tube around the city for a little while and stop in all the stations. I find the tube stations fascinating now.

"I never really paid attention to them before. I have been taking them my whole life so I just never paid attention to it, you know?" I say

"Well I've never been here before and I think they're great now that I know I won't die in there. Some of them are total tourist destinations, like Kings Cross and Paddington station. But some of them are more understated." We're reaching St. Paul's station now. We start to walk out of the tube station, and as we're about to leave I stand at the entrance of the tube station when he suddenly stops me with a nervous look crossing his face, when he suddenly leans in and kisses me. His lips are soft, and his kiss starts off as hesitating, like he doesn't want to make the wrong move. Soon though he pulls me in closer and kisses me harder, with a wanting hunger. He smells vaguely like a cologne I can't place. He places his hand gently on the right side of my neck and pulls me closer and I melt in to his arms. He catches me off guard and I don't exactly know how to respond after that but to smile at him and take his hand. So it was like that we walk onto the tube and held hands the whole way home.

~ ~ ~

Tiana is still up when I get home.

"There you are, finally," she says, "tell me all about it."

"We won," I smile.

"I don't care about the game. How exactly was the date."

"I'm not telling," I say and put on my headphones so I can ignore her constantly asking for details. I'm not sure if Duncan and I are together now, but I sure hope so.

Fleur

I knock on his apartment door and quickly look around, hoping no one saw me come in here. I only stand there for a few seconds before he opens the door.

"You're here, finally."

"Why the fuck are the curtains open? Zut." I walk up the the window, look out briefly to make sure there isn't a security camera out the window and close the curtains long black.

"We've been doing this for years and have never been caught. Calm down, babe." He sits on his bed in his satin black robe.

He might want me to call him Richard, but he will always be Mr. Barnes to me.

He starts by unbuttoning my dress. The pink satin fabric falls to the ground and I step out of it, leaving n my black leather heels because I know how much they turn him on. He's already laying on the bed in his boxers. I turn my back to him and walk toward the bathroom. It's partially out of necessity - I have to get ready - and partially for the show for him. I pump the lubricant in to my hand and apply it to myself. Half of the trouble with my job is getting them to believe I actually want it. Which twenty two year old in her right mind wants to sleep with her middle aged teacher? None of them, but if I've learned anything in this world, it's that you have to do some things you don't always want to do. I try to get in a sexy mood, and go back out there and do my job.

"You're so fucking hot," he says and gently pulls my hair. *Il vaut mieux etre rapide.* I'm straddling him, still wearing the heels. My feet are starting to hurt but I don't let my face show it. I'm wearing the blue baby doll lingerie piece he asks me to put on, and I'm glad I get to wear something this time. It still allows access to all my important parts and he thinks I'm wearing it for him. I feel his hot breath of my breasts and I try to enjoy it. I close my eyes and I can almost imagine it's someone else. I make sounds to make him think I'm having fun. I've been told men can tell when you're faking, but so far I've been good at acting. Because I'm that - an actor - and this is no different form any other role I've done.

When he thinks I'm finished I get on top of him, and spend the next few minutes making him think I'm satisfied and I want him to be too.

In under an hour the whole act is done. Curtain, bow, thank you, and good night.

I get my tip for the night and get back to the campus as quickly as possible.

"Where were you?" Cathy asks me when she's standing outside the campus for a smoke.

"Nowhere."

"You must have been somewhere."

"I just went out to a cafe to study."

"Okay, okay." She puts up her hands in surrender. "What are you doing tonight?"

"I don't know, studying and rehearsing probably."

"Oh, please. You know you don't need to do any of those things. You get all the best roles."

I wonder if she knows what I've done to get all those roles.

"I still need to practice, you dumb twat. *Zut. Allons-y.*" I turn and leave with a wave of my hand and she snuffs out her cigarette. She smells like crap, I hate those damn cigarettes. Cathy and I go up to our room and I spray some air freshener. I wish I had chosen to room with Rosie, but I know she snores and I didn't realize Cathy picked up that nasty habit. My computer beeps with a message from Papa.

Which role did you get?

I think it's actually him this time and not his secretary pretending to be him. I can tell because he asked it like a real bastard. At least the secretary tries to make him sound loving. Some x's and o's, a hello and goodbye. Papa just gets the information he wants.

Portia, I response

And what is that? You know I haven't read that overhyped bull crap.

The lead I say. Not exactly the truth, but he'll never find out about it, and it might shut him up for now.

He logs off without another comment. I wonder if he knows what I've done to make it here. So what if I only get a role as an extra, or one with few lines? At least with his support I wouldn't have to fuck my professor. But I don't have that, so here I am.

"Have you heard about Duncan and that Canadian bitch?" Cathy asks.

"What about them?"

"They're dating."

"Like, officially?" I pull out my compact mirror and start reapplying my MAC Snob lipstick.

"Yeah, obviously."

"Slut. I bet she already fucked him."

"I bet he's paying her."

"*Quelle?*" I ask as my head snaps around and I stare at her.

"I think she's secretly a hooker. You know, has some madame or something. She probably thinks she's a classy call girl. Never know, she could have fucked one of the profs to get here."

I try to keep my face straight. Is she serious? Does she think Olivia is having sex for money? I hope she isn't. I don't like Olivia much, but I wouldn't wish this on her. I remind myself that I can't tell my friends what I have done to get here. They would never understand.

"What if she is fucking one of them? It wouldn't matter to you. *Merde.*"

"She's probably full of diseases and shit. I wouldn't talk to her."

"You can't get an STD from talking to someone, you dumb shit." I pick up my tote bag with my school books and go to the study room. I'm probably losing brain cells by being in the same room as that bitch.

Chapter Fourteen

> My tongue will tell the anger of my heart, or else my heart concealing it will break - The Taming of the Shrew, William Shakespeare

I have another visit with HR in their office that Wednesday.

"We've been reviewing your case. We really don't want this information to get out," Mrs. Anderson says.

"What do you mean? If he did something that was illegal he needs to open up about it. We can't fix it if everything is kept a secret," I say.

'I understand how you feel..." This fucking bitch. No, she does not know how I feel. She has no right to say that. "But this is the way it works, Sweetie." *Bitch.* "Just pretend like nothing happened and I'll take care of it.

"I can't do that. How am I supposed to live and work in this kind of an environment? He keeps saying things to me I don't like. And I know Fleur has still been acting funny. I'm not sure she has stopped doing what she was doing."

"Well, considering that no one will tell me what exactly that is, it's none of my concern. Just let me do my job and you look pretty and pretend that nothing happened." She flashes me a fake smile indicating I have to leave her office.

"What's wrong?" Tiana asks when I stomp into the room. I gave her a recap of our conversation.

"I hate that woman," she says. "You need to avoid seeing him though".

"I know. I still want something to happen to Fleur because of what she did though."

"It's okay. we'll make it all work out. You have to go to rehearsal. He'll probably be there, so try not to think about it and just be safe," she says.

~ ~ ~

I love rehearsal but it's three hours a day I have to spend with Fleur and Mr. Barnes in the same room. The biggest problem with her being the lead, in my opinion, is that she has to be in every minute of rehearsal so I have to do some double acting. I have to memorize and perform my part and at the same time act like I don't know what Fleur is doing and pretend that Mr. Barnes isn't sexually harassing his students. On the up side, I also get to spend it with Duncan. He is a great actor. And a great kisser. I smile as I see him practice.

Duncan as Shylock practices his aside, "How like a fawning publican he looks!
I hate him for he is a Christian,
But more for that in low simplicity
He lends out money gratis and brings down
The rate of usance here with us in Venice.
If I can catch him once upon the hip,
I will feed fat the ancient grudge I bear him.
He hates our sacred nation, and he rails,
Even there where merchants most do congregate,
On me, my bargains and my well-won thrift,
Which he calls interest. Cursed be my tribe,
If I forgive him!"

Fleur practices the next scene for the second time today. I'm yet to practice.
Fleur as Portia says,
"In terms of choice I am not solely led
By nice direction of a maiden's eyes;
Besides, the lottery of my destiny
Bars me the right of voluntary choosing:
But if my father had not scanted me

And hedged me by his wit, to yield myself
His wife who wins me by that means I told you,
Yourself, renowned prince, then stood as fair
As any comer I have look'd on yet
For my affection."

"That's really wonderful, guys. I'm happy with how this is coming along. There are a couple of little things I want to iron out later, but for now let's just skip to scene three and get some other actors a bit of practice," Mr. Barnes says. Finally, I know I am going to get some practice. I am determined to outshine Fleur.
I, as Jessica, begin,
"I am sorry thou wilt leave my father so:
Our house is hell, and thou, a merry devil,
Didst rob it of some taste of tediousness.
But fare thee well, there is a ducat for thee:
And, Launcelot, soon at supper shalt thou see
Lorenzo, who is thy new master's guest:
Give him this letter; do it secretly;
And so farewell: I would not have my father
See me in talk with thee."

"For the most part that was great. Olivia, we'll work on it," I hear Fleur and Rosie snicker behind me.
I sit down on the bench with Duncan and he puts his hand on the small of my back. It is a small gesture but it helps. We finish up the first day of rehearsal and I am feeling pretty defeated.
"Don't worry about it, I'll practice with you," Duncan says.
"Thanks. I could use your help. I'll go to see Mr. Barnes later, too."

"Are you sure you want to do that?" He knows how uncomfortable I am around him.

"What other choice do I have? I have to get better or I have no hope of coming back."

"I just hate how he's doing this to you," he says, "I want to protect you."

"I can protect myself," I say.

"I know. You're a strong girl. I'm sure you don't need me for this type of thing but still I want to be there for you."

"I'll be okay. Look, I'm going to go over there now and I'll come see you right away when I'm done and let you know how it went."

"Okay, be safe." He gave me a kiss before I left. I feel a rush in my head and a fluttering in my diaphragm. I'm not sure I'll ever get used to that, but I would like to try it out more.

I knocked on Mr. Barnes' door.

"Hello, Olivia. Come in," he says when he opens it.

"I need some help with a scene," I say.

"I'm surprised you came."

"Excuse me?"

"Don't act stupid. I know people and they told me what you did and how you betrayed me."

"Who told you?"

"That doesn't matter. I thought we had something special here."

"What did I do to give you that impression?" I ask.

"You told me you want it. You told me with your eyes and your glances, your body gestures. I know you want me," he says and reaches for my hand.

"No, no Mr. Barnes. I don't." I reach my hand away and stand up, trying to leave. Before I know it I am pinned against the wall and am struggling to break free of his grasp.

"Don't you dare leave. I made Fleur do what I wanted and look where she is now. One of my best students. I have you in my grasp and I won't let you go," he says, "you're a beautiful, beautiful woman." He strokes my hair. It would have been a romantic gesture if it wasn't so unwanted. He plants his lips on mind and forces my mouth open with his. For just a moment he is only holding me by one hand. I take this opportunity to lace my fingers through his shaggy hair on each side of his head and clamp my fingers shut tightly, and knee him in the groin, sending him doubling over in pain. I run through the door and don't stop until I get to Duncan's room in a fit of tears.

I tell him everything that happened with Mr. Barnes.

"I'm going to kill him," he says as he gets off the bed and heads to the door.

"Please don't do anything stupid. I already had Kenneth put the camera in his office. I'll get him to give me the footage which I can bring to HR. it might be a fight, but I'm going to make it happen. Just let me take care of it, please."

"Fine, but I don't really want you going near him while you're alone. You know someone in each of your classes, so get them to walk there with you make sure you and Tiana always lock your doors."

"I know, and I'll be safe. I hate that I have to protect myself from him. I don't want to be afraid of him but I can't let him hurt me."

"Whatever happens, just know that it's not your fault. None of this is your fault, and I'll make sure he's held accountable for what he did."

He gives me a hug and we lay down on his bed I clutch his t-shirt and ball up the green fabric in my hands. I feel like I'm begin torn apart, but also so safe and secure in his arms, I never want to leave.

"I want to talk to them. My parents," I tell Duncan and Tiana. They've been weary of leaving me alone for a second. We agree that they can wait in sitting area in the corner of the hallway. I tell them they can't listen, that I want privacy and they agree and leave.

I start to get hot and sweaty. I know this feeling, this has happened before. I try to resist but find my way to the bathroom. I carefully crouch on the clean white floor. I can vaguely smell the lemon cleaner I know Duncan uses in his room every Sunday. I carefully put my finger in my throat and heave up the little I have in my stomach. I make a horrible retching sound and taste the sour vomit coming up the back of my throat. I think for a minute how there is no way Duncan and Tiana aren't going to notice the smell, but I don't care. I go in to the bathroom and quickly kneel down as close to the toilet bowl as I can get so I make sure to keep quiet. I finish bringing the content of my stomach up, I glance at the clock. It's been ten minutes already, and I have no idea how long he'll be gone for. I quickly clean up the bathroom, spray air freshener, and use some mouthwash. I don't want to tell my parents what happened, but I feel like I have to. I have to tell them it happened again.

With shaking hands, I lift the lid to my lap top and click on the video chat app on my screen. I take a few deep breaths and motion Tiana to leave the room. I don't want her to hear this, even though I know she'll just sit in the hallway with her ear pressed against the door anyway. Still, I don't know how this is going to go so I don't want an audience. After almost a minute of agonizing wait, my Mom answers the video chat.

"Hey, Mom," I say quietly, trying not to show my emotions.

"What's wrong, Sweetie?" She asks. I see her on the computer screen sitting at the dining table with a cup of coffee in front of her and her hair up in a messy bun. She has her leftover makeup still smeared on her face. She obviously hasn't gotten her shower yet this morning. When I lived at home she had a daily lecture from me about not washing off her makeup before she went to sleep, she only washed it off in the shower in the morning. Sometimes it felt like I was the parent more than she was. We were more like friends than mother and daughter. I should have known I wasn't going to get anything past her for a second.

"Is that Olivia?" I hear my Dad ask from the kitchen. He peeks around the corner in to the dining room, drying off a plate. Looks like they just finished breakfast.

"Hi, Dad." I wave to the camera. Dad goes back in to the kitchen and comes back out a second later without the dish and pulls up a seat next to Mom.

"What's wrong?" Mom asks again.

"I just... had something kind of weird happen. I just wanted to talk to you about it."

My parents share a look of shock and uncertainty and I go on.

"It's... one of my teachers. I don't want to tell you everything, but it was on the news last night so I don't want you to see it online or anything. He kissed me, and tried to hurt me."

"He did what?" Mom shrieks at the same time Dad asks, "Olivia? That was you?" Dad asks.

"We saw an article on Facebook. Aunt Jackie shared it. They didn't name the victim. I mean to call and ask if it was one of your friends. They said there was an investigation or something, but oh, god... I didn't think for a second it would be you."

"I'm going to kill him," my Dad says through clenched teeth.

"Dad, please..." I try to say before my Mom starts wailing. She starts sobbing and grabbing Dad's shirt. He begins rubbing her back and comforting her.

"Mom? Mom, get a grip!" I say in to the computer screen. I wish I was in the room with her so I could shake her and make her get it together.

With a loud sob Mom forces herself to stop crying and finally look at me. She looks slightly embarrassed but is still an emotional wreck.

"This is not about you, Mom. Don't pretend it is," I say.

"It is a little about me, Olivia."

"Dad," I look at him for help and he looks down in his lap.

"Don't be so selfish, Olivia. Do you know how hard this is for me?" She says.

"Selfish? *I'm* being selfish?" I want to lower my voice, I'm sure half the hallway can hear me yelling, I don't care. I can't believe that after all these years she hasn't changed. "You. Fucking. Bitch."

I see the shock in my parents' faces as they fall utterly silent.

"What can we do for you, honey? Do you want to come back home?" Dad asks, finally having some empathy in his voice.

"No, Dad. I don't. I'm not coming home. I've worked too hard to be here. I'm not giving up my dream because of him. I want to take legal action... I think. I don't really know yet. But still, I'm going to stay here."

"No, Olivia. It's not safe for you to stay there."

"Dad, it's fine, really."

"How did this happen, Olivia?"

"I don't want to tell you all the details... I mean, I just went to his office hours and he trapped me. I got out before anything major happened but still. It was scary."

"What did you mean you *might* take legal action?" Mom asks.

"I mean I'm talking to a legal advisor and might charge him or something."

"How is this a might? He needs to be put away," Mom says.

"Guys, I'm taking care of it."

"Why not? Just say that he did it to you. Make him take a lie detector test or something. You can't let him get away with this."

"It's not that easy."

"It doesn't have to be easy. Nothing is easy, but sometimes you have to do it anyway."

"I think I know a little about that."

"What, is it about the eating disorder? So what, Livi, you skipped a couple of meals and went to the hospital for a few months. It's not that big of a deal. I would love it if someone told me to gain weight."

I can feel the hair on the back of my next start to rise. She can't do this to me. Not today.

"I should have known you guys weren't going to help me. Just like last time."

"This is nothing like the eating disorder," Mom argues, "You did that to yourself. There was no one else at fault there. Now you can finally save some other girl by putting him in prison."

"That's not what I meant by 'last time'," I finally say.

"What?" Dad asks.

"It was Michael," I spit, "Michael touched me. When we were kids."

And once again, I bring them to silence with a revelation.

"Why didn't you tell us this sooner?" Mom asks.

"I tried to. You guys didn't really want to sit down and listen. And it was hard, I thought it was my fault."

"It wasn't like that. You didn't always tell us the truth when you were a kid. We didn't know what to believe. Michael denied it. Who were we supposed to believe?" Mom asks.

"Well, it wasn't your fault," Dad says to break their silence, "I want you to know that."

"I know this story with that…teacher, if you can call him that, is going to go public, but… I don't want you to mention Michael in any interviews. There's nothing we can do about it now, and Jackie doesn't need his memory tainted. Please," Mom pleads.

Of course that's Mom's main concern. The family's image. How Jackie will feel about her precious boy.

"You know we're worried about you, and I want you to get some professional counselling when you get home, but know that I'm proud of you. You're going to make it really far in life if you continue to not let people walk over you. You're doing well, Sweetie," Dad says. I'm glad they aren't trying to make me leave, because I never would have gotten on the plane back home. I started something here and I am damn well going to finish it. After I asked Mom and Dad not to tell John what was happening quite yet. I don't want him to worry.

I turn off my computer and put it on my nightstand and curl up with my brown bear, named Brownie, who my Dad brought me when he and Mom brought John home from the hospital and I was only four, and I start to sob. I hear someone open the door and feel Tiana's soft hands under my shirt and gently rubbing my back. She stays there for the rest of the night when we both fall asleep.

~ ~ ~

"We have some things to talk about. Alone." I tell Kenneth as I'm standing in the hallway outside his door.

I look at his roommate and clear the space by the door. Thankfully, he picks up the book he's reading and leaves without a fuss.

"I installed the cameras a week ago. I didn't look at the footage, I didn't know if you wanted me to or not," Kenneth says.

"I'd rather you didn't watch them. I don't want you to see that," I say.

"That's okay, I understand. That's my computer there," he points to the small desk he had that was the same as the one in my room, "my headphones are next to it, too. The cameras have been there for a couple of days so you'll want to speed it up a lot to weed out the parts you don't want. You can also skip to a certain day if you want to." I thank him, put the headphones on my ears, and start with what I know I need to see.

I skip to yesterday on the tape and see a clear view of my teacher sexually assaulting me. I try to hold back tears as I watch the tape but it's hard. Seeing it is like letting it happen all over again. I can tell Kenneth is worried about me but he doesn't say anything. I cut that part of the video out and save it as a separate file on Kenneth's desktop. I move onto the next video.

This one is a little less exciting. I speed the video up so it only takes me about half an hour to get through each day, but I know I will be there a little while. On the third day, though, I see something of interest.

I see Mr. Barnes walk in the door and presses play to make the video go at the normal speed. I see he and Fleur speak for a minute, he hands her something, and they go over to her bed and started kissing. I speed it up again, not wanting to see this whole exchange. Part of me feels bad for invading Fleur's privacy so much but this is unbelievably immoral for a teacher and a student to do. I watch the rest of the encounter but nothing else happens. They talk for a little after and he leaves. I curse the lack of audio on the tape, but Kenneth says this is the best he can get with such a small camera. We can't risk getting caught. I cut that video out and email both of them to myself, and removed the two separate videos from the desktop. I want to keep the whole of the original files on Kenneth's computer and trust he wouldn't watch them. He and Harper seem to be getting along well and he doesn't seem like the kind of person to mess up a good relationship over something like that.

I take the files straight to the HR department.

"Olivia. I'm glad you're here, I was discussing your case with the local police and some of the administration here at the Globe. This is going to be a very hard battle for you and I am unofficially recommending you stay silent about it. It's what's best for you." How does this random woman know what is best for me?

"With all due respect, I have evidence of the assault and I will be pressing charges," I say.

"Yes, well. Once you make a statement to the police, you may not be able to stop with that process. They'll make you go through with the court proceedings. It may take years."

"I'll speak to the authorities in both the UK and Canada and I will make sure I have a full understanding of my rights. I will not be taking legal advice from a woman with a bias for an attacker." I stand my ground. I am not about to let this crazy woman control me. God only knows how many women Mr. Barnes also attacked, but that doesn't matter anymore. What matters is what I can change now, and I can prevent him from doing anything like this in the future.

"I have evidence and I want to make a statement. I would appreciate if you showed me where the local police station is so I can make that statement." She gives me directions, and I go to the station with Duncan.

"I'd like to make a statement about a sexual assault," I say to the woman at the front desk. She has her brown hair pulled back tightly and is wearing a perfectly crease-free police uniform. She has empathetic looking brown eyes. She seems like the type of person the police force needs.

"Yes, of course. Just let me go get someone," she says. She seems like a nice lady, I wish I could tell my story to her.

"Hello, I'm officer Logan," a tall, balding man holds his hand out to me, then Duncan.

"I'm Olivia. This is my friend, Duncan. He's not directly a part of this but I'd like to have him for support. Is that okay?" I ask.

"Of course, as long as he behaves himself and doesn't cause any trouble," the man laughs, "we have someone here for the both of you for support as well. She's a volunteer from the local sexual assault crisis centre. Would you like her to stay with you? She can help you through the process of the statement and you can talk to her after you're done if you want to."

"That would be nice. Thank you," I say, and he guides me into the small interview room.

"So this is going to be somewhat informal, but note that what you're saying is being recorded so we can reference it later. Please just tell me what happened, in your own words," he says. I tell him what happened between Mr. Barnes and I.

"I also have some evidence, actually." I pull a flash drive out of my purse, "I know it's totally weird, and probably illegal, but I hid cameras in the rooms of the people involved after the first harassment experience. I brought the recordings for evidence." I slide the flash drive across the table.

"There are two files. One is the sexual assault against me, one is something generally suspicious. It's a sexual encounter between a teacher and a student. They exchange something, and I think the student in the video is selling sex. I don't want to get her in trouble. I think he's the problem. I overheard a conversation between the two people in the video and it sounded like he was making her do this so she could further her career. You have to make him stop," I plead.

"Thank you for this. We'll take a look and begin an investigation soon. You did the right thing today, Ms.

Williams. I want you to have this card," he says and slides a purple business card across the table. There's nothing written on it but a 1-800 phone number and a picture of a purple and teal butterfly, "this is a sexual assault crisis hotline. They're not connected with the police, and everything you say will stay between you and the volunteer. I've been told talking to them can help out a lot."

"I don't know. I feel like all I've been talking about to people has been this assault. I don't want to burden someone else with hearing about it, either."

"They're volunteers, that's what they're there for. And you don't have to call, but I think it would help," he says.

We take the tube back to the Globe with the business card clutched in my clammy palm. I know I'm going to call when I get back, but I don't want to think about actually talking about it again.

I'm a little shaken from telling him my story so it's hard to start talking to the volunteer when I actually work up the nerve to call.

"Hi there, my name is Mallory. These experiences can be hard to relive, so I'm here for you.

"I know what happened wasn't my fault or anything, but I still feel bad about it," I say.

"Bad how?"

"I feel like he shouldn't lose his job after this. Not even for his sake, though, but because he's good at what he does and he really does give people good opportunities."

"But he chose to do those things to you. He is a grown man who should be responsible for his own actions."

"I feel bad that I'll get Fleur - one of the other students - in trouble. I don't even know if what she did was wrong, but she can't be given favouritism. And like I know Barnes sleeping with his student is illegal, so there's no way she could have given consent to him."

"What happens to or between them isn't up to you. You told the authorities the truth, so it's up to them to press charges or not, and it's up to Fleur to seek help if she feels she needs it. All you can do right now, Olivia, is take care of yourself. You seem to have great supports in your family and in your friends, and the other students in the program who believe you. Keep people like that around and you'll be okay. You're a strong girl, I have faith in you."

When I hang up I decide I need to clear my head so I start on a light jog up the Thames to cool off. Luckily, it's right before sunset so I get to enjoy the breathtaking view of couples holdings hands and boats making their way across the river. It is a warm night in July and the sky is splattered with pink and orange hues. It is as perfect an evening as I could have imagined, and I was able to just run, Mr. Barnes taking up no space in my mind for the whole hour, which is all the therapy I need to continue on with my summer.

Chapter Fifteen

Listen to many, speak to a few - Hamlet, William Shakespeare

Duncan, Tiana, and I sit around the television watching the news. We all want to watch a movie but James insists he watch the news first. I like to keep up with politics and social events so I thought I would enjoy getting in touch with the world outside the Globe again, but I really didn't ever think I would be on it.

The young female news anchor says announces, "next up we have an interesting story from the Globe

Theatre. As a part of the summer study program students have come from all over the world to study there and perform at the end of the summer, one lucky student will be getting a contract to work there for a year. One of the students was not so lucky, however. We have reports that at least one, and possibly more, young women have been facing sexual harassment from the professors there and human resources has been trying to keep it under wraps. Our inside source says that so far nothing has been done to reprimand this teacher and he still holds a position of authority over the students. We have no word yet on the identity of the victim or the perpetrator but we will keep the public updated on this story as soon as we have new information."

Everyone in the room turns and looks at me, no one saying anything.

"Well, I think we know who their source is." I finally break the silence.

"What do we do now?" Duncan asks.

"That flowery bitch," Tiana says.

"We should give them what they want."

"Olivia..." Duncan trails off and I walked out the door.

I have no idea where I am going. Do I go to the BBC offices? Where are they? Instead I walk up to my room and get online. I find the story tip line and decide that is good enough for me so I used the phone in my room to call and introduce myself.

"Hello, yes. I'm calling in response to the news I saw today. About the sexual harassment claims? Well I was one of the women harassed and I would like to bring the real story to your attention." We set up a time and place to meet and I start preparing for my big television debut. Everyone knows I'm getting in contact with them so word gets around quickly that I was going to be on the news the next day.

"Olivia, you don't need to do this," Tiana says as I'm getting ready.

"Why wouldn't I? I'm not ashamed over what Barnes did to me. They're not planning on doing anything about what happened and they're going to regret it," I say. I picked my bag up off the chair and leave. If they aren't going to support me I am going to go on my own. No one fucks with Olivia Williams and gets away with it. I make it to the cafe early and order a coffee, waiting for the reporter to get here. I bite my nails in anticipation but stop as soon as she walks in so I can at least attempt to have an air of confidence.

Eventually a woman in her thirties who is dressed in black dress pants and a silky purple top walks in holding a microphone with the BBC logo on it and a man holding a large black camera is walking behind her. She sits down at the table across from me.

"Hello, Olivia, right?" She asks.

"Yes, that's me," I say.

"Hi, my name is Joanne Jones," she says, "I'm pleased to meet you."

"Hi, it's good to meet you, too."

"Just so you know what's going to happen here, I have to ask you to fill out this consent form." She slides a sheet and a pen towards me. "I'm going to ask you a couple questions, and you're going to answer them as best as you can. Please don't name the teacher yet, we have someone working on getting that information released. We're not allowed to mention who he is on air yet. Also if you know of other victims you can tell us that but don't name them either. We don't have a release form they have signed and we want to avoid that lawsuit. Sound okay?" She asks.

"Yeah that sounds okay." I sign the form.

"Good. Let's get rolling," she says.

"I'm Joanne Jones with BBC One reporting from London with a follow up with yesterday's story. One of the victims of the sexual harassment case at the Globe Theatre has bravely come forward and is willing to speak to me about what happened to her recently. Coming to you with the news first, we have Canadian Olivia Williams." The camera pans to me.

"Olivia, please introduce yourself." She holds the microphone to my lips.

"I'm a second year university student from St. John's, Newfoundland. I came here for my first trip to England and was really excited to study at the Globe this summer."

"Well I'm glad you're here and I hope your experience doesn't colour your image of this beautiful country. We're all dying to know, what exactly is happening behind those walls that the general public knows nothing about?" She asks.

"No, I'm still glad to be here and I will return in the future. I went to his office so I could get some help going over my lines. He did help me but then was acting kind of creepy. You know, putting his hands on my stomach and not letting go when I asked him to. I didn't think much of it until the next time I went for help. He said I was his property and if I did what he wanted I he could get me far in the theatre world. I said no and tried to leave. He pushed me up against the wall and assaulted me. I was able to get away but now I, and most of the other young women who work there, don't feel comfortable going to classes every day."

"I totally understand why you wouldn't want to go anymore. I know you can't mention who he is but could you please tell us what is happening in terms of reprimanding this man?"

"As far as I can tell, nothing. He still works there and I still have to see him on a regular basis. The authority figures there haven't been cooperating with the victims much."

"Awful, just awful." She wraps up the interview with some closing remarks and the cameras are turned off. I can finally breathe somewhat comfortably again.

"That was really great, Olivia," she says, "this is going to be a good story. Let me get your contact info just in case we need to do a follow up story. News has been slow lately." I give it to her and leave the cafe to go home. I manage to keep it together for the duration of the interview, but when I leave the cafe I can't help but release a few sobs. I bend over in pain as if someone has just stabbed me in the stomach. I have the urge to purge again, and remember the coping techniques I was taught when I was recovering the last time.

1...

2...

3...

4...

5...

I count to 100. I take a deep breath and straighten my back. I slowly start walking down the Thames, deciding to walk home to clear my head instead of taking the tube. I take a deep breath in through my nose, so big my belly fills up with fresh air, and slowly let the air out my mouth.

100...

99...

98...

97...

96...

95...

When I reach 1 again, I wipe the tears away, and the urge to purge is almost gone completely.

When I get home everyone is surrounding the television in the common room with the news turned on. I know why they have the news turned on, an obvious difference from the throwback movies and Disney animated films that are normally playing on a loop in the ancient VCR. People are sitting on the sectional couches that surround the television, and papers and text books are covering the coffee table. Everyone is trying to finish up their group work and research papers, all while not missing the news story.

"Guys, the story won't be on for a couple hours yet," I say.

"I know," Tiana says, "I just wanted to start watching now just in case they started playing it a little early. I still can't believe you did that."

"Well, I did." I sit down at one of the desks in the far side of the room and put in a pair of headphones so I can focus on writing my paper until the interview airs.

Twenty minutes until air time I put away my things and sit in front of the television. I really don't want anyone to see me right now but I want to see what they did with cutting the interview and it would be a while before it goes up online.

We all watch the interview and it is basically as I expected it to be. They have me speaking and cut to some shots of tourists walking around outside the Globe.

Once it's over everyone look at me expecting a reaction. I don't give them one. Instead, I go upstairs.

Duncan follows me.

"Babe please talk to me," he says, "are you mad at me?"

"No, why would I be mad at you?" I ask.

"Honestly, I didn't totally support your decision to go to the media about this whole thing. I don't think it's going to help."

"Yeah, I know." I bury my face in my pillow. He lays down next to me and begins gently rubbing my back.

"Tell me about it," he says.

"You already know what happened."

"I know but you didn't tell me how you feel about it. Are you scared? Nervous? Want to talk about it? Just want to forget it happened?"

"I feel... used. And betrayed. And also like it wasn't that big of a deal and that some people go through things so much worse. Like, I shouldn't complain about it, you know? But at the same time I don't feel comfortable here or rehearsing, or in classes. Everyone knows what happened and if Barnes gets fired they're going to be pissed. He has a lot of connections and can do good for the production. But he can't do that to me and get away with it," I say.

"That's a lot to deal with," he says.

"Yeah I know."

"I wish I could do more to help."

"Stay with me tonight?"

"Yeah, of course. I'll let James know that I won't be home tonight and I'll suggest that Tiana stay there, too," he says and kisses me on the forehead before he pulls out his phone and had it arranged.

So there we stay for the night. I don't want to move so we don't even change into pyjamas, I just remain in the jeans and t-shirt I wore that day while we fall asleep in each other's arms.

Fleur

"*Zut*. What the fuck was that?" I ask when he opens his apartment door.

"Maybe you can tell me. Did you tell them? Did you go to the media?"

"Me? No, of course not." I try to keep my face neutral.

"You're lying to me. You fucking bitch." He slams me up against the wall and pins me down. He forces his mouth on mine and opens it with his tongue. I bite down quickly.

"UHHHH," He moans before punching me in the rib. I collapse in pain and he follows me to the ground. A few drops of blood spurt out of his mouth and on the floor next to me. He quickly takes off my dress and unzips his jeans. I try to shove him off me but he holds my arms down.

"I will fucking kill you." The rage in his eyes makes me believe him. I close my eyes and go limp, hoping it's over quickly.

When it is over, he tucks my hair behind my ear. "Here, get up now. I don't want you crying. Why are you crying like that?" He helps me up and takes me to the bathroom. I flinch when the wet face cloth touches my skin and wipes the tears away. I take a deep breath and try to compose myself.

"I can do it now," I say and take the cloth so he'll leave me in the bathroom alone. I turn to face the mirror. The bruise on my ribs is already developing in to a dark purple colour. *Aie.* I muster up all my courage and turn around and face him.

"I'll go to the hospital. They'll believe me, I swear. I know what to do after a rape."

"What rape? It was no different than what we've done before."

"You're wrong. I'm going to press charges." I stand up and start putting on my shoes.

"Come here. I have to show you something." I recoil when he puts his hand on my lower back and guides me away from the door and toward his computer. He opens a folder in the documents section of his computer.

"This is from when we met," he says and begins scrolling through the numerous emails we've exchanged. He has all of them. "And here's our phone conversations." He plays a short audio clip.

"Hey, just wanted to make sure we were on for tonight…" I hear my own voice reverberate from the computer speakers.

"And here's my favourite," he says and opens a video clip. I quickly close my eyes and plug my ears. I know what he's play and I certainly don't want to see or hear it. I had no idea he was recording everything we said and did together.

"I… I have to go." I grab my purse and slip on my sandals and spring out the door. I can hardly get out of the building and to the nearest trash can before getting sick on it.

"Fleur?" I hear someone ask behind me. *Fuck*. I straighten up and walk quickly in the opposite direction on home.

"Fleur," I hear Tiana say and she puts her hand on my shoulder.

"Get the fuck away from me."

"You're sick, you need help."

"*Je ne dois rien vous.*"

"You know I don't speak French. Please, speak to me in English."

"I. Don't. Need. Anything. From. You."

"Please, Fleur. We used to be best friends. I'm worried about you." I finally turn to face her. Her face is written with hurt and worry.

"Look, I'm sorry. I've been dealing with a lot right now and I just don't know how much I can talk about it."

"Can you try? For me?"

No matter how much we fought when we were friends, she was always there for me when I needed her before.

"I'm not telling you what happened."

"You don't have to. Let's just talk."

"So. How have you been... doing?" Jesus Christ this is so awkward. When will she let me leave.

"James misses having you around."

"I really don't think any of your friends care about me. I hear you, you know. When you're all snickering when we're in dining hall. You think I can't hear you, but I can. I hate it. I pretend to be okay with hanging out with Cathy, Mary, and Rosie, but they're so awful."

"They've always been awful. I have no idea why you chose them to be friends with."

I laugh, "because they're the only ones who didn't hate me after you stopped liking me. God, they're stupid. And so easy to manipulate. You walk with confidence and show them something shiny and all of a sudden they'll do whatever you want them to.

"Why can't we be friends again? Why did we even fight?"

"Because we - I - was too competitive. You were successful and I hated it. I was stupid and only wanted to surround myself with people I knew I was better than. I always want to be the best, and I can never let it go."

"Then try. Try to let it go. I know you can. Just come hang out with us some time. I know Duncan liked you more than you realize, and Harper can see the good in any one."

"And Olivia?"

"And Olivia and I will still stay friends. It'll be okay."

"I can't. I know you want me to, but I can't be friends with her. At least not now. Not this summer." I think about how she went to the media. She told my story before I did. She had no right. She can only speak for herself. And from what I hear, all Mr. Barnes did was try to kiss her. She doesn't understand what I had and how she ruined it. She doesn't understand how her opening her big mouth hurt me.

"No. Honestly, Tiana, I can't be seen talking to you. I need to leave."

"Wait, here," she reaches in to a pouch in her purse, "take this. Some Gravol. It will make you feel better."

"*Merci.*"

Chapter Sixteen

Love comforteth like sunshine after rain - The Complete Sonnets and Poems, William Shakespeare

Harper, Tiana, and I sit in The Muse holding large cups of iced coffee and with lap tops open on the table in front of us. We're all researching for our term papers and trying to keep cool. We're all wearing cotton sun dresses and sitting as close to the window as we can, to try to catch a breeze. This week has been abnormally hot, even for summer. The Muse doesn't have air conditioning because it's so rarely needed in London. My skin has felt hot and sticky for the past three days, and I cringe to think of the sweat stains that are gathering on my clothes in the most unflattering of places.

"How are you feeling about everything?" Harper leans in and asks me and waves a fan she made out of note book paper in front of her face.

"Like what?" I ask and swat a fly out of my face that came in from the screen less open window.

"Well you've been through a lot this summer. How are you and Duncan doing?"

"We're good. I think we're going to make it work long distance for a little while at least. I don't want to plan for forever with someone and end up with my heart broken but still I need to try to make it work with someone I feel so strongly about."

"Makes sense. I know it didn't work out between the two of us but everything happens for a reason. I was his first real relationship after Meg, it was kind of like a practice relationship for him, you know?"

"Yeah I know. Every relationship is different," I say.

With her eyes still closed Tiana says, "My cousin was in a long distance relationship with her boyfriend for three years in college. They're married and have like a dozen kids now. And that was even before Skype. Could you imagine?"

"Nope, I could not imagine that."

"And Mr. Barnes? Are you feeling okay? It would be normal to feel really traumatized after harassment or an assault like that."

"The word *assault* feels so extreme," I say.

"He touched you without your permission and even used his authority over you to make you feel scared and like you couldn't make it stop. That's assault. He didn't stop after you asked him too, that means it was harassment, too."

"Well everyone knows who he is and what he did now so maybe it will keep him from doing something like that again." Tiana says.

"I still wish he was going to be charged," I say.

"The court process is also long and extremely exhausting. You could have to stay here instead of going back home, which means putting graduation on hold or transferring to a school here. And even then it's very rare that he would actually be convinced without any physical evidence. It's your word against his."

"Would they not believe me?"

"Some people would. Some people would see him as a very well respected man and you as a student who was jealous she didn't get the lead role."

"Yeah. Especially when they like Fleur so much, it's a mystery to me why."

"She puts on a face for the camera. She's an actress. it makes sense how she can fool them so easily." I say.

"That's true." Tiana says.

"I hate that Jenna and Steven are broken up because she's so torn up about it, but I am so glad I never have to see Max again. I know now that just because someone helps you when you're down, I seriously don't need him or owe him anything." I say.

"That's my girl." Harper gives me a hug.

"You'll be okay. I Promise," she says.

"As long as you guys come visit me in Canada sometime. If you don't I will not be okay."

"I wouldn't dream of not doing it." Tiana says.

~ ~ ~

"How did you find The Muse? It's kind of a hole in the wall," I say, looking around. Duncan and I are each holding a mug of green tea and drafts of papers for revision in front of us.

"Yeah the person that showed me this place was really great. We were close,"

"Was? What happened?" I hope I'm not crossing a line by asking.

"It was my first real girlfriend. I had gone on dates and casually dated a couple people in high school but I was really focusing on getting in to a good college so I didn't want to have a serious relationship so young. I wasn't looking to fall in love with her but with someone like that you couldn't help it. She really was a one in a million."

"Tell me about her."

"I met Megan in the most average way anyone could imagine. It was the first day of University and everyone was moving in. All the first-years full of hope that their University experience would be just as good, if not better than their high school experience.

I had a pretty mediocre high school life. I got decent grades but wasn't the top of my class. I had friends but I wouldn't have considered myself popular. I liked sports and did well on the football team but wasn't the MVP. All in all it was pretty unremarkable. The only remarkable part of my life was Meg.

"On move in day at uni, I was just getting everything straightened away. I was putting up my Chelsea poster – that same one that you've seen above my bed, actually – and she came in.

'Hey, I'm Megan Bell. You can call me Meg. I live next door, just thought I would say hello.' I knew I was hooked when I saw her beautiful smile. 'So everyone is coming out to a party on third floor tonight. You coming?'

'Yeah. Of course. Yeah, totally, I'll be there.' I was nervous but couldn't not go. I was determined to have a good freshmen year.

'Great. My roommate and I are leaving around eight, so you can meet me in my room then if you want and we can go over. Have you met your roommate yet?' She looked over at the other side of the room. Everything was put away neatly but my roommate, which housing had told me was named Mark but I hadn't met yet, was nowhere to be found.

'No. I think his girlfriend has an apartment nearby or something. I don't think I'll be seeing him much.'

'Okay. Well, see you later… what was your name again?' She asked.

'Duncan. I'm Duncan Doyle.'

'Oh, alliteration. I like that. Well I'll see you later, Duncan Doyle.' She went back to her room. But she kind of…floated. That's always how she walked.

So I went to the orientation icebreakers and stuff that fill up the first day but I didn't see her again until that night. I changed into jeans and a blue polo shirt. I knocked on her door and her roommate opened it. They were playing some techno music I hadn't heard before and Meg was spraying something, which I have gathered was probably hairspray, on her hair. She was wearing a fitted red dress and her long black hair was curled.

'Hey, Duncan, this is my roommate, Julia. Julia, this is Duncan. Let's go.' She took a couple bottles of cider to bring upstairs.

First we danced at all the fast songs. I wasn't much of a dancer but we sure had fun. Eventually we danced together for all the slow songs too. And I knew I liked her. At the end of the night I walked her down to her room to say goodbye. It killed me not to kiss her because I knew we both wanted to but I didn't want to come on too strong. I knew she was different from the girls I had dated in high school so I had to tread lightly, this was new for me.

The next day we went to the movies. It was a simple first date but I knew we would both enjoy it. We were together from that point on. We had a wonderful year. I was planning on asking her to marry me after graduation. It would be a while away, but I wanted to live with her for a while first. She was more of the romantic but I was more of a realist. I knew I wanted to be totally ready before I asked her that.

Eventually I got a call from her Mom. She could hardly speak. I knew something was wrong and I asked where they were. She said they were in the hospital. It wasn't far from school so I ran there. I could have driven but parking would have taken too long. When I got there I was out of breath but the person at the desk actually managed to understand me. I walked into her room and her parents were surrounding the bed, holding hands. She wasn't moving but the machine next to her bed was beeping steadily so I knew she was still alive.

Beep.

Her head was bandaged but I could see the dried blood under the dressings.

Beep.

She hit her head against the window during the crash.

Beep.

It was someone not paying attention and he ran a red light.

Beep.

Turned out the driver survived and was texting someone that he was going to be late.

I spent a lot of time with her family until she passed. Her Mum and Dad and I didn't leave her side for the weeks she was in a coma.

Beep.

It was medically induced, they were hoping she would heal faster that way. Her body healed well, but her brain never would have survived that kind of trauma. She would have been in a vegetative state forever.

Beep.

We all knew that's not what she would have wanted from her life. It was a hard decision to take her off life support but they had to do it.

Beep.

She and I were planning a future together and she told me that if anything ever happened to her, she would have wanted me to end her life peacefully.

Beep.

She really valued her mind and not being able to learn anymore would have really been torture. We both agreed early on that if anything happened to us we wanted a death with dignity.

Beep.

She also told me that she didn't want me to mope around if she died. I didn't take it seriously at the time because I didn't think anything could happen to her but I was wrong.

Beep.

So there I was, with my girlfriend's family, about to turn off the machine that was keeping her alive.

Beep.

I'll never forget that day. It was the worst day of my life."

Beeeeeeeeeeeeeeeeeeeep.

I can't say anything back to him. I just hug him. I know he's trying to keep me from seeing him cry. I'll never tell him I can feel his tears on my neck.

Chapter Seventeen

My tongue will tell the anger of my hear, or else my heart concealing it will break - The Taming of the Shrew, William Shakespeare

"Oh. You," Fleur says, scowling at me when she opens her door.

"We need to talk," I say.

"Do we? You know, I really don't think there's much I can say to someone like you. *Au revoir,*" she tries to close the door but I stick my foot in the doorway at the last moment. That's what they all do in the movies so it seemed like a good idea at the time. What they don't tell you when they do that in the movies is how much it fucking hurts.

"I need to explain myself, I know. So please let me do it," I say.

"Fine. You have five minutes," she says, arms crossed in front of her chest.

"Okay. Well, first I overheard you two on the day of the auditions, like bargaining something. It was weird but not too weird. And then he made me uncomfortable. And then I kind of… got someone to install cameras in your room and his office…"

"You did WHAT?" she yells at me, "I. Am. So. Fucking. Mad. That is a complete and total invasion of my privacy. I should have you arrested, you little bitch!"

"I know, I know. I'm sorry. I just had to have evidence that he was hurting students, so I thought…"

"No, you didn't think. You obviously didn't think about anyone but yourself. Everyone knows you're just doing this for the attention. You went to the media as soon as someone gave a shit. You're just using this for the attention so people will feel bad for you and give you work so they can feel better about taking on some dumb charity case," she accuses.

"I know what I did was wrong but that accusation was completely out of line. I did nothing like that, and you know it. I knew from the moment I overheard your conversation that you were giving out sex to further your career, which is *way* worse than what I did. At least I was protecting myself, and yes, even you, from him. I didn't like being shady and sneaking around, but I had to do it."

"I still can't believe this. Everyone is going to know what I did." Fleur flops down on the edge on her bed and put her head in her hands. Oh god, what have I done? First I piss her off and now she's crying. I'm a little afraid this is a rouse to get me to come closer to her, and she could proceed to choke me, but then I realize it would be nearly impossible to get a body out of her room without someone noticing so probably she won't risk it.

"Fleur, please, I'm so sorry..." I tentatively put a hand on her back and try to comfort her. This was the worst job I have ever done at comforting someone but it is the best I could muster.

"I can't believe I let this happen," she says.

"Let what happen? This isn't your fault."

"I just wanted to do well. My parents already don't support me, and I need to make sure I'm the best so I can land the best roles and prove to them that I can do it."

"But it's your life. You need to live it for you."

"What did your parents expect you to do after high school?" she asks as she looked up at me.

"Nothing, really. They just kind of... let me pick, I guess."

"See, there you go. Your parents are supportive of you no matter what. Mine aren't. I know I'm privileged to come from a family with money but people don't know what it's like. Papa came to France with nothing built his life from rock bottom and now he has a whole empire. It's completely a disappointment for him if he had a daughter who is mediocre. I need to be the best or work for him, those were the options. They would have liked me to do film because it's more obvious to the general public. They want to see me on movie screens and be able to point that out to their friends. Doing small theatre work won't be good enough for them."

"So you decided to sleep with someone to get a lead role?"

"He approached me, actually. He knew who my Dad was. It's pretty common knowledge that my Dad has zero respect for the arts, even though he runs the companies that provide the camera, lighting, and sound equipment they need. His products are the best so they're used all over the world. Anyway, Barnes knew what a dick my Dad was and we started talking. I told him too that my Mom had no backbone and she would never stand up for me. That's when we started getting closer and spending more time together when I was here over the summers. I knew what I was doing was wrong but I did it anyway. He eventually gave me the idea that I could use what I had to get further in life. I knew that it would kill me but I would do it if I had to. I did, and it wasn't so bad. I did it again, this time asking for money too, and he did. I realized I could get pretty much whatever I want. I don't regret it or feel bad though. I'm only going to do it for as long as it takes for me to be able to make it on just performance work. You think I'm different from you, but I'm not. You would do it too if you had to." I really doubt I would ever go that far, but still I have never been in that situation. I hate Barnes for manipulating her, and then me. I have no idea how many women he did that to, but I knew it is stopping this summer.

"Oh, I almost forgot. If you ever need anything, these people are really helpful." I hand Fleur the card that the police officer gave me. I've been keeping it in my wallet, just in case I needed it again. If everyone who volunteered for them was as helpful as she was, I know that Fleur can get help from them.

~ ~ ~

I get a phone call from the police the next day.

"Olivia, hello, I just wanted to update you on the case. Do you have a moment?" the man asks.

"Yes, I do."

"Okay, we've spoken to Mr. Barnes and he's decided to surrender his position at the end of the summer. I know this means you have to be around him for another couple of weeks, but we have rules in place to ensure your safety. We know the media already knows about the situation but we really need to keep this quiet, it's for everyone's best interest. I'm not technically supposed to discuss another person's case with you, so off the record, Fleur will not be facing charges for what happened with her. She cannot give consent to a person of authority so it has been decided that she was not in the wrong here. We'll send someone over to patrol the campus and make sure you feel safe. Mr. Barnes will not be allowed to be alone with a student. If someone needs to see him in his office, the officer will be there with him. The other staff members have been briefed on our safety measures and have agreed to report any suspicious activity during group rehearsals. If you have anything more to report, you have our number. If it's an emergency, you can always call 999."

    "Thank you for everything, really. I appreciate it more than you'll ever realize," I say.

~ ~ ~

    The summer is coming to an end, and we know we are going to get really busy in the next few weeks, so the program coordinators have organized an end of summer party. Tiana and I are getting ready with Harper and a pop hits playlist is pounding from Tiana's speakers. We're all about the same size which is lucky for us because it means we get to borrow from Tiana's closet. I end up wearing a tight blue dress with a plunging neckline and black shoes with a small heel, which normally would have been much too much for me but I think I might as well try something new tonight. Harper is wearing a more conservative black dress with cap sleeves and silver flats, and Tiana went all out in a long, gold, sparkly gown complete with 6 inch tall black leather pumps. I let Tiana do my makeup and she goes with a dark smoky eye and a light lipstick, and she kept my shoulder length blonde hair sleek and straight. I hope Duncan doesn't think it is too much but I feel confident and sexy. We're going to meet the boys at the party. The coordinators have the inside of the Globe done up like a club, serving drinks and strobe lights everywhere. We're some of the first ones there so we're there before the boys.

"This is the first and last time Tiana will be ready before I am," James jokes as he comes over and gives her a hug.

"Olivia," Duncan smiles and offers me his hand.

"Duncan," I say as I take it and we begin walking away from our friends.

"How am I so lucky to call you my girlfriend?" He asks.

"Can you?" I joke. He hasn't actually asked me to be in an exclusive relationship yet. I know we both consider ourselves a couple but I thought it would be fun to joke around with him before I let him make it official.

"Why can't I?" He asks.

"Well, we have not made any particular agreement," I say.

"Humph. I'll have to arrange something," he smiles and kisses me, "there isn't anyone else is there?"

I pretend to think about it for a moment. "You know, there used to be. I don't think you have to worry about him any more though." I slide further into his arms and continue kissing him and we dance slowly before the song changes to a faster one.

"Oh, I love this song!" I say and start dancing.

Duncan shakes his head as he mouths the lyrics to me.

"There you two are," Harper exclaims once she finds us again. "I've been looking everywhere for you. I know you're all in love and stuff now but seriously we need to all dance and have fun together," she pulls at my hand and drag me across the dance floor, Duncan turning around and walking towards the bar to get us both drinks. He joins us again and I take my drink, dancing in a circle with our friends.

Chapter Eighteen

Though she be little, she is fierce! - A Midsummer Night's Dream, William Shakespeare

"You're aware we have a paper due this time next week, right?" Harper asks as she sees me reading in the common room.

"Yes…" I put my book back in my bag and take out my laptop. I have yet to finish the paper, let alone edit it.

"I've been slacking so much on papers and stuff lately," she says. I know Harper is an overachiever when it comes to grades, like I am. If we don't do well on the paper it is going to be the end of us but I can't exactly focus on the history of performance when Duncan always wants to hang out in The Muse with me. I can't say no to that guy if I want to.

"We both need to focus for at least a little while," she says, "I don't want this trip to be the reason I don't graduate." Good point. I pull up the screen with my paper and spend the next couple hours finishing my first draft. When I finish, I stand up and stretch out my arms.

"Finished or quitting?" Harper asks.

"Both," I say.

"I hear you."

"I'm done for now, but I want to go for a walk to get some exercise before I start editing."

"Good plan. You can leave your things here, I'll be camping out for at least another hour," Harper says.

After about ten minutes of walking through the winding streets behind the Globe, I jump when I hear my name.

"Olivia!" I hear someone shout and see Mr. Barnes jogging towards me. I turn and walk in the opposite direction, trying not to panic. "Wait," he puts his hand on my shoulder and I spin around.

"What do you want now?" I ask him, "you know what you did was wrong, and I have no problem pressing charges if you do anything like that ever again. There are police around here somewhere, I'll scream. I'll call 999. I'll kill you."

"Woah, hold on. I am not in the wrong here. Look at you, what you wear around here." I look down. I'm wearing a denim skirt and a white tank top. It's the middle of summer so I don't think what I am wearing is wildly inappropriate. I would nearly melt if I am not wearing this.

"There is nothing wrong with what I'm wearing," I say, "There's something wrong with you for acting creepy around a student. Now please, if you try to speak to me again I have pepper spray and I will use it." I don't actually have any so I pray he doesn't give me a reason to use it. I make a mental note to get some though just in case.

He lets go and I calmly walk away until I know I am out of his sight, then I begin running to Duncan's room. I barge in the door and he looks up at me from his desk with a concerned look on his face.

"Please don't tell me he said something to you again," he says.

"I just was walking…and…he, he grabbed me." I say crying hysterically. "He didn't hurt me but I. Was. So. Scared." I try to speak more but begin choking on my words.

"Do you want to come to my Harlow with me this weekend? It's a town in Essex, where I grew up. I know you're busy so you can bring your computer and books for your research paper, but I would love it if you could come and meet my family before you have to leave."

"I would love to," I say.

"Great. I'll get our train tickets soon and we can leave Friday morning." I am glad we don't have classes on Fridays. It leaves a lot more time for weekend getaways which I have been doing often lately.

I'm so excited to meet Duncan's sister. He said she's coming home for a week in between visiting family around Europe and we have just handed in a couple of our assignments so we decide that it is the best time to go home to his place. I worked extra hard on the remaining assignments and was able to free up a couple of days where I don't have to do any school work. I am nervous to meet his family but I think they will probably like me. It is also strange to be staying over there for a couple days even though we have been only dating for a few weeks but it was now or not for a long time. We decide to just do it now.

We get on the train early in the morning and get there pretty quickly. It's only a fifty minute train ride to his hometown. He talks about his family on the way there, hoping it will keep me from getting too nervous.

"You'll love my sister, Darcy. She's a lot like you, loves everything artistic."

"How old is she again?"

"She's eighteen. My parents shouldn't be there for too long. Dad's at a conference right now. We're not sure when he's supposed to come back, could be any time. Mum is in full production mode so she'll be at the office or the theatre for most of the days we're here and come back to get something to eat and then crash."

"Were they gone that often while you were growing up?" I ask.

"They were home a little more often but mostly we were raised by housekeepers. I forget the name of the person they have now. They were always finding something wrong with the person and firing them before I could really get to know them. I spent most of my time with Darcy. The only stable thing we had was each other."

"That sounds hard," I say.

"It was. It was great to have parents who were successful in their careers and stuff but it didn't leave time for them to raise kids."

"Why did they have you two? Don't get me wrong, I love that you and Darcy exist but it doesn't seem like they had the life for kids."

"Mum is great but she's forgetful. She never remembered to take the pill."

"Twice?" I ask incredulously.

"I guess so." He just shrugs.

"I'll try not to make that mistake." I try to lighten the mood. I think pointing out that he and his sister are unintentional pregnancies will probably not keep him in a good mood for long.

We have to get a taxi from the train station. His house isn't big but it is very nice and cozy. A Victorian style two storey made of brick with a nicely manicured and fairly large garden on the front and I could see another large garden with trees at the back of the house. A young woman, who must be Darcy, with red hair and freckles opens the door and waves at us.

"Duncan!" she throws her arms around him. She isn't much younger than he is but she is almost a foot shorter. He has wildly curly red hair, unlike Duncan's dark brown.

"Hey, sis." He hugs her back. "This is Olivia." He gestures to me once she let him go.

"I thought so. Darcy." She stretches her hand out to me and I shake it.

Duncan shows me around the house. It's spotlessly clean except for Darcy's room which is littered with clothes and shoes on the floor, the books are stacked on the floor, desk, and unevenly on the bookshelf.

"Okay, that's enough of judging me based on my messy room." Darcy closes the door and follows us to Duncan's room.

I should have expected what I saw but I didn't

It's blue.

Everything is blue.

The walls are blue, the bedspread is blue and white plaid, the furniture is navy and there is Chelsea Football Club jerseys on hangers covering the walls.

"You know I'm a fan…" he says.

"I should have seen this coming."

"You really should have."

"Did you not warn the girl?" Darcy asks, "you need to inform her of the extent of your crazy."

"I wear the shirts almost every day and brought a poster with me even though I was only in London for a couple of months. She should have seen it coming."

"The only thing that would make you seem more obsessed is if you dated someone named Chelsea," Darcy says.

"I'm really surprised you haven't," I say.

"Okay, okay, enough of this. Everyone out of my room." He points to the door.

"This is where you'll be staying." He opens the door at the end of the hall. It is your average guest bedroom, yellow themed and neat and tidy, I lay my bags down by the bed.

"Now let's go for a walk or do something," Duncan says, "no need in staying inside all today, it's really nice out."

The two of us go for a walk down the road. He insists we stop first at an ice cream shop around the corner. I look at the sign that looked homemade and stated it was "Mabel's Milk Bar" and they have homemade gelato.

"What's your favourite kind of gelato?" Duncan asks me.

"I wouldn't know. I haven't had it before." He looks at me like I have two heads.

"Excuse me?"

"It's not big in Canada." I shrug.

"Why would they keep you in such a deprived state like that?"

"I don't know. Fear of hypothermia if we consume cold food in the winter?"

He pretends to think about it for a moment.

"Makes sense. We wouldn't want to risk it." He opens the door for me and rings the little bell. The shop is small but the big windows facing the road make it look much larger. All the walls, tables, and chairs are white, and the counter had a row of delicious looking gelatos, a menu above the counter advertises hot chocolate and flavoured coffees. There aren't many flavours of the gelato but the pistachio looks amazing so I go with that one. Duncan gets the black raspberry cheesecake. We take them outside and sat at a little table with a big white umbrella over our heads.

"This is flawless," I say as I take another bite.

"So I doubt I could convince you to move to the UK for me, but what if I promised you gelato every day you were here?"

"That, I would consider," I say as I take the last bite.

We continue walking down the road and he was talking about all the places we were walking by.

"That's where I went to school." It is just time for classes to let out so I see all the kids dressed in little blue and black uniforms running out of the building and towards buses or cars. It's rare for kids to wear uniforms in Canada but I learned it is very common here.

"So you've lived here all your life?" I ask.

"Most of it. I was born in London but Mum is from Harlow so they moved back when I was pretty young. I spent all my school years here though."

"That's cool. I moved around a lot as a kid. Dad was always going to different cities to work so we followed him around."

"Did you find it hard to change schools so often?"

"It wasn't as bad as you would expect it to be. It was hard at the time but I kind of like it now. I got to make a lot of friends, and if it wasn't working out in one school I knew it was only a matter of time before I moved away and got to start all over again."

"I wouldn't mind starting over again," he says. "I've been looking at schools in Canada, you know. There's a med school just about everywhere. I should be able to get into Memorial's based off the grades I've been getting so far, and I have some good references lined up."

"I know you could get in anywhere you want," I say.

"But would you want me there?"

"I would love to have you there with me. Either you and Jenna and I can find a place that will fit all of us, or maybe Jenna will meet someone else by then and we can move into a place with just the two of us. I would love to see you every day," I say.

"I'm glad. I really like you," he says. "I could see myself with you for a long time, Olivia."

"We'll just take it day-by-day for now and see what happens. A year is a long time for things to change or finalize. Who knows what could happen."

We end the day with making dinner for his family. I meet his Dad pretty soon after dinner is ready so I hope cooking for him helps to make a good impression on him. His Mum eats at the theatre. She's so tied up with work it's hard for her to come home sometimes. I am told she just comes here to sleep and gets up to leave again before anyone else was up when it is busy like this. It is good though that she is busy. She is widely regarded as a great director but I knew that theatre was a dying art so jobs were few and far between in the last couple years.

They were able to maintain their comfortable lifestyle with the money his Dad made but sometimes were hard for them.

We decide to end the night with Duncan, Darcy and I watching a movie.

"We're watching *Clueless,*" Darcy says as she reaches for the DVD.

"There is no way I am going to let you put Olivia through that," Duncan says. They both look at me to make the decision.

"Clueless is fine," I say, I'm not particularly excited about the prospect but there was no need to make his sister hate me. She spends most of the movie talking anyway so I can pay attention to her instead of it.

"So tell me more about living in Canada," she says, "is it always cold there?"

"No it isn't, Darcy. Don't be stupid. They have summers too," Duncan says.

"It does get super cold in the winter though. Depends where you live, too. Canada's a big country. The climate can change with where you are in it." I shrug.

"That's cool. I would love to go there," she says, "maybe a road trip. If I flew to Newfoundland would you drive to British Columbia with me?"

"I love you but you couldn't pay me to stay in a car with you for all of Canada," Duncan says.

"You're not invited," I say. Darcy smiles at me.

Duncan puts his arm around me and I snuggle into his chest. Darcy sticks her tongue out at him and turns to watch the movie. It doesn't take long for me to fall asleep in his arms. He wakes me up at the end of the movie and we go upstairs to our separate bedrooms to get some real sleep.

Chapter Nineteen

All the world's a stage, and all the men and women are merely players - As You Like It, William Shakespeare

After dinner we get ready to go see his Mum's show. It's good timing that her production is on the last day we were in Harlow so it gives us something fun to do before we had to leave again. We both get dressed up to go to the show, and I still have no idea what we are going to see. I love surprises.

It's a small theatre and it was decorated in blue, black and silver. It is obvious why Duncan likes this one so much. He fits right in with his black dress pants and blue dress shirt, and he is wearing a tie with the Chelsea

Football Club logo on it. I should have suspected he would have something like that on.

"Ready to see my Mum in all her glory?" He asks me.

"Ready as I'll ever be." I whisper to him as the curtains open.

It begins with thunder and lightning, and I know what it is. *The Tempest*. I haven't read this yet but the premise always intrigued me. I'm so excited to love it. I squeeze Duncan's hand, I'm not entirely sure how he knew that I wanted to see this one but I'm glad he did. I get swept away in the show. The costumes, the acting, the special effects, and of course the directing, are all perfect.

"How did you like the show?" Duncan asks once it's over.

"I loved it. It was amazing," I say.

"Would you like to go backstage?"

"Of course!" I should have considered that he would be able to do that considering his Mum was running the show. We wait for the other audience members to clear out first, and then we get up and walk across the stage to get to the backstage area. I had no idea behind the curtains there were two staircases. One going from the audience to the stage, the other going from the stage to backstage. It's a great setup, very easy for people to move around in.

It's loud back there and everyone is putting away instruments and talking excitedly.

"Mum! There you are," he says when he finds her and gives her a hug.

"Hello, Olivia. I'm so glad you were able to make it. How did you enjoy the show?" She asks.

"It was so beautiful," I say, "you're a very talented director."

"You're too kind," she smiles warmly at me, "I like her, Duncan. Maybe you should try looking at medical schools in Canada. Never know what could happen." My heart flutters at the idea. I have to keep reminding myself it's only a year until he finished his degree and could go to a new school. I can do a year long distance. I know I can.

"Dad has a big dinner planned to celebrate the premiere. Any idea when you'll be home?"

"Soon, honey, I promise. I just have to get some things cleaned up here first. The cast part isn't for another week when the performances are over so I'll be home tonight."

We leave and begin walking home.

"Something is up with them," Duncan says.

"Like what?"

"I know you don't know them so you don't know how different they're acting. Darcy mentioned it to me yesterday. She says they've been fighting a lot lately. he just got back from the conference this morning and they've already been getting in a fight."

"About what? I know that times can be tough sometimes. My parents fight, too."

"About nothing. And everything. I don't know, like simple things. Like not doing the dishes the right away or not having dinner made for when Dad comes home even though Mum was at work all day too and just got in the door herself."

"I'm sure they'll work it out."

The dinner seems fairly normal to me but I also know that I don't know the whole story. They mostly ask me about myself and where I am from.

"So, Olivia, what are you doing in school?" His Dad asks.

"Performing arts and English."

"Major and a minor?"

"Double major."

"Nice" his Mum says. At least I know *she* likes me.

"I guess," his Dad says. Uh, that *can't* be good. Duncan shoots a glance at his Dad. We continue with dinner, talking about nothing in particular until it is finally over. Darcy, Duncan, and I all go to Darcy's room to discuss what is going on with his parents.

"Something's wrong," she says as soon as we close the door.

"I think so too," Duncan says.

"Have either of you just asked about it?" I ask.

"I did but Dad denied anything," she says.

"Well maybe it's financial problems. I know the economy is rough right now and money can be stressful. Any chance it's something like that?"

"Maybe."

We hear a knock at the door.

"Guys, can we come in?" I hear Duncan's Dad ask. He opens the door.

"If you don't mind, Olivia, we'd like to speak to Duncan and Darcy alone for a moment."

"Yeah, sure, no problem." I get up and go in to the guest bedroom. I take a book out of my suitcase and try to read to no avail. I am too nervous waiting for Duncan to come to my room with some sort of news.

I hear voices and a door slam from downstairs, and someone stomping up the stairs. Duncan opens my door.

"Tell me what happened." I sit on the edge of the bed and patted the spot next to me. Instead he lays down a gestured for me to lay down with him. I do, and wrap my arms around him.

"They're splitting up," he says.

"I'm sorry." I have no idea what else to say.

"They have to declare bankruptcy," he says, "I guess Dad has been having some problems lately. He's been drinking a lot and gambling. Mum has been doing really well at the theatre, all of the money she would put into a joint account. Dad's responsible for paying the bills so she didn't notice right away that things weren't getting paid for. They have to move out of the house. They're going to lose just about everything."

I don't know what to say in response to that. I just hold him close and rub his back until it is time to go to bed.

"I wish I could stay here for the night," he says.

"Me too. But your parents don't want you to stay here. I promise you can as soon as we're back in London and in the campus."

"Okay. Thank you for being here for me. I know this is not the fun weekend trip you wanted or expected but there's nothing I could do to make it better."

"I don't care where we are or what we're doing. I just want to be with you." I kiss him.

It's some as we get ready and leave the next morning. We all know his dad would be moving out into an apartment as soon as he says goodbye to Duncan, and Darcy still has to stay here and help her Mom pack up the house. We board the train and he falls asleep as soon as the train starts moving. I sit there for the full ride with my arms wrapping around him, wishing I can make it better and knowing I have to leave soon. I wish he could have something stable for a little while.

Chapter Twenty

Do you not know I am a woman? When I think, I must speak - As You Like It, William Shakespeare

"Hi, Olivia. I'd like to speak to you," Mrs. Anderson says when she calls my room phone.

"Okay, I'll be down soon." I go down right away, knowing she wouldn't page me for nothing. I'm able to walk straight into her office without waiting.

"Hi, sit down." I do.

"So as you know, we have approached Mr. Barnes about your accusations numerous times. You know he still denies what happened but after the media coverage he was a little afraid of his name getting out and having it hurt his career. So anyway he has decided to resign from his current position. You'll go the rest of the term with Marcus as acting director. He is very skilled and I'm sure you'll be okay with this," she says.

"I… I really didn't want to get him in trouble." What am I saying? I want him to get whatever was coming to him. I have to keep reminding myself he is the one who was in the wrong, not me.

"Others have come forward with information. He has done this to more than one student. Some of them are talking about pressing charges if he doesn't have some sort of punishment for what he has done."

"What did he do to other people? And how many people has he victimized?"

"I can't tell you the details for confidentiality reasons but some people had it worse than you did. You didn't meet them. Most of them didn't come back."

"But how many were there?"

"Five in addition to you and Fleur."

This is awful. Some girls apparently had it worse than I do. What happened to them? I don't think I want to know. That could have been me so easily.

"I've changed my mind. I've spoken about it to my friends and family and I've decided that I don't want to press charges but I can't just let him do this."

"Are you going to release his name to the press?"

"I don't think so. I don't think that's my job. If someone else wants to do it they can and I'll support them, but I don't want him here anymore."

"I was planning on speaking to him soon and encouraging him to step down from his position."

"Good." I leave her office. I feel confident in my decision. She speaks to him and fairly quickly we are informed he will no longer he directing the final performance. He's going to wait until we were all gone before he moved his things out of his office, though.

When I leave it's time to get ready for our final dress rehearsal. We have done so many regular rehearsals but a couple times we got to do the whole performance in costume, which was always fun. We're still a bit of a mess, especially because we're all so nervous, and this year we have to do everything without a director we can trust.

I go in to the costuming room and walk over to the section that normally holds my dress. Huh. It isn't there. I continued shuffling through the racks of clothing looking for my dress. I make it through the side of the room which holds all of the women's costumes. Frantically, I begin shuffling through the men's clothing. Nothing. I go over to the shoe closet and tore everything out when Harper walks in.

"Olivia, what are you doing?" She asks.

"My dress, I can't find my dress! We perform in a couple of days!"

"Oh shit. Hold on." Harper runs out of the room to get Mrs. Kent, head of costuming.

"Olivia can't find her dress…" I hear her explain as the two of them walked into the room.

"Where did you put it last?" She crosses her arms and looking down at me condescendingly.

"I shipped it back to Canada so I could steal it before I even got to wear it. No. Where do you think I put it? I put it back on the hanger in the wardrobe, where it belongs, so I could find it when I needed it today."

"Well no one has been in here all day but you. Either you didn't put it back or it disappeared. Either way, you need to find it before we have to return the costumes or you're going to have a nasty bill to pay at the end of this." I can feel my pulse begin to quicken. No. I can't do that. I'm planning on starting to save up as soon as I got home so I can maybe visit Duncan next summer. No way can I afford whatever gargantuan fee that I would be charged for the fancy gown.

"Go get the others." I instruct Harper and point to the door, "we're sending out a search party. We have to find that dress."

I get any and all students I can to help me find the dress and section us off to different parts of the theatre and campus, and Mrs. Kent agrees to check Mr. Barnes' old office for us. He hasn't cleaned it out yet. We all know what happened but no one says anything. We all know I didn't lose it or forget to put it back. Someone took it and hopefully hid it somewhere, and didn't destroy it. I've made many friends over the summer and have made many enemies as well. Some people thought that Mr. Barnes did nothing wrong or thought I'm lying. Others are friends with or admire Fleur so they hate me by proxy. I have to check the backstage of the theatre, Tiana is going to check in the dress shop to see if someone just returned it, Duncan is going to check the common areas, and Harper is checking the rooms of anyone who will let her in. It takes over an hour. Everyone is frustrated that we're wasting time that should have been spent rehearsing, but we can't get far with the dress rehearsal without the dresses. I'm beginning to lose hope when suddenly the search is over.

"I found it," Duncan exclaims as he comes into the costuming room. I'm half looking around the backstage of the theatre and half having a panic attack. I'm sweaty and beet red, my heart nearly pounding out of my chest. This is one of the worst things that can happen to me right now. I look at him with the blue dress draped over his arm that he was stretching out to me. He looks beautiful. I mean, he looks good most days but here he is, saving the day. But he is always the one who helped me when I need him the most, which was often this summer. I take the dress from his arms. It's a little wrinkled but other than that in perfect condition. My costume jewellery is still nowhere to be found but that, I can replace.

"Thank you!" I jump into his arms, and he proceeds to swing me around and kiss me.

"Puke," I hear Harper say from the other side of the room, "I know you guys are all adorable and in love, no need to show the rest of us."

"Sorry." Duncan laughs, unapologetic, and knowing that Harper is joking. "Sometimes I find this girl hard to resist."

We all know who the culprit is. Fleur is innocently eating dinner when we were all looking for my dress. She strolls into rehearsal ten minutes after we finally start.

"Did I miss anything?" She asks me. I'm appalled she has the nerve to say anything to me after what she knew she did. People are looking at us so I try to keep myself together.

"Nothing. We were just discussing how wonderful the dress looks on me." I do a little twirl. I can't believe I've just done that but I can't just stand back and let her walk all over me. Obviously speaking to her like a regular person won't work so I have to sink to her level. It's not something I'm proud of, but something I did anyway. By now everyone has turned away from us and continued their conversations. I lean in to her and whisper in her ear.

"Do anything funny like that with me again and I will destroy you. I already have the guy you want and am better at acting than you are. Mess with me again and you'll see how bad I can make this for you." I smile at her and walk over to Duncan and kiss him on the cheek. I don't turn around to look at her but I can feel her eyes burning into the back of my head.

We finish up rehearsal and Duncan and I decide to go to The Muse first instead of going straight to bed.

"I can't believe she took your dress," he says when we sit down with our teas.

"I know. She's crazy."

"I knew she liked me but I didn't think she would take it out on you like that. I'm so sorry, Olivia. You were so afraid," he says.

"It's not your fault." I held his hand over the table. "She chose to do that. Harper dated you for a while and still doesn't hate me. It's her problem, not ours."

"Should we talk about what's going to happen next with us?"

"What do you want to happen?"

"I want to be with you for as long as I can."

"How long do you expect that to be if we're apart?"

"I don't know. You know it didn't work out with Harper and I."

"Well I don't want you to sit here and make all kinds of promises only to decide it doesn't work out a couple weeks after I get back. I'm done with not knowing where I stand with people. Either you are going to try your hardest to make it work or I'm done."

"That's fair and I respect you more than that. I mean, I respected Harper too. No, that's not what I'm trying to say. I love you, Olivia."

"I…"

"I know it's too soon to say that but it's true. I really do love you, Olivia. I want to make it work and I will make I work. Because we belong together and distance can't change that."

"Have you been speaking to Jenna lately?" Duncan asks. We're sitting in the on the floor of the common room with binders and papers spread out in front of us, trying to get some homework done.

"Yeah. She's still planning on coming in for a couple days to watch us perform so it will be good for you two to meet."

"I'll be looking forward to it."

"She and Steven are still broken up. At first I didn't think she would be able to not see him when he called her back. I knew he would call her wanting to go out again, it was just a matter of time."

"So did he?"

"He did. He came up one night and she more or less slammed the door in his face."

"Good for her," he laughs.

The next day we begin classes again with a frenzy. We have papers to hand in and presentations to do before we are able to perform. When I first heard about the program I knew we would be taking classes in addition to the performance but I didn't expect it to be this busy. Tiana is spending all her time in the sewing room sweating all over fabric. Not all the dresses that we borrowed fit perfectly so it is up to the fashion students to alter them appropriately. I decide to see if I can help her try to feel a little better.

"You need a break," I say as I drop off some coffee, a bottle of water, and a donut at the table.

"You know you can't bring food in here, right?" she says. I exaggerate looking around the room. We're the only ones here.

"I think I can fend off the crowd of crazy fashion students. Oh wait, that's just you." I reach into my bag and pull out a donut for myself. She reaches for the coffee.

"How many cups have you had so far today?"

She counts in her head for a moment. "Five. Not including this one." I take the coffee from her and put the bottle of water in her hands.

"You need to have this first. You can have one coffee for every bottle of water."

"I didn't sleep last night."

"I know. Which is why I'm enforcing this rule."

"You're cruel," she says and takes a sip of the water.

"It's just because I love you."

"Okay, you need to leave. You're distracting me." She tries to shoo me off her desk.

"I have news about Jenna and Steven," I say and take a sip of the coffee.

"Okay, you can tell me that. And then you need to leave."

I fill her in on Jenna rejecting him.

"That's wonderful," she says, "I hate that guy and I haven't even met him."

"Well you wouldn't like him any more if you did meet him. If I never saw him again it would still be too soon."

"What are you going to do when you get back home? Your school isn't very big so you know you'll see them there. You even have some of the same friends."

"Well I could transfer schools and make all new friends, but maybe that would be a little drastic."

"Just a little."

"I'll just have to get used to seeing them around and not letting it affect me. I know that I was the one who broke it off with Max in the end. You know that he kind of offered to hook up again when I got home but there was no way I was going to do that. So I am planning on just ignoring them whenever I see them around campus."

"Sounds like a good plan."

"Unfortunately that's all the gossip I have."

"Then you need to get out of my sewing room so we can both get some work done. I know you just came to visit me so you can procrastinate." She's right.

Duncan and I spend the night in his room, and James in my room with Tiana. We all decide we need to relax for a little while and just hang out and watch movies together. Duncan and my relationship has been escalating quickly so I knew I was ready for a more serious physical relationship, and I feel like he does too.

"Are you sure you're ready for this?" Duncan asks me. We are laying on his bed.

"Yes, I'm ready." I take my shirt off and begin kissing him. I run my hand through his hair and he gently tugs my hair out of my ponytail. He turns me over and lays me down on my back. My heart rate begins to increase as he unbuttons my pants. I do the same with him.

When we are both in our underwear he looks me over carefully, like he wants to appreciate what he sees. He kisses me and gently bites my lip and begins moving his kisses downward as he carefully unclips my bra and then takes off my underwear. I've never felt this beautiful and appreciated before. I have had other sexual partners, some I was committed to and others I was not. But this is different. It's at this moment that I knew I was in love with Duncan Doyle. I feel his breath hot on my thighs.

I know he is going to be there in the morning, which makes the night so much better, and we fall asleep in each other's arms

I wake up the next morning to roll over to see a beautiful, though very disheveled looking, Duncan.

"Good morning beautiful," he says with a crack is his voice, it is clear he had just woken up as well.

"Hello handsome." I kiss him.

"Olivia, I love you," he says. He looks confident, though he's quiet.

"I love you too, Duncan." I say and he kisses me. I bury my face in his chest and fall asleep again for a little longer.

Chapter Twenty One

What's done cannot be undone - Macbeth, William Shakespeare

"So what happened last night?" Tiana asks the next morning. She and I went to The Muse for breakfast so we could talk alone for a little while.

"It was great. The best night I've had for a while."

"That's good but I didn't ask how it was. I asked what happened," she says.

"I am not telling you what happened. I just want it to be for the two of us."

"Just tell me and then promptly forget you told me."

"Nope. Sorry."

"Damn."

"How's the costuming coming?"

"It's good. We managed to avoid a real crisis with your dress. But other than that I've been sticking myself with needles constantly while trying to get the minor characters' costumes and doing the alternations for the major characters." I cringe at the thought of Tiana sticking herself with a needle. I *hate* needles.

Tiana and I spend the morning going over my lines and how I can improve my performance. I'm using every opportunity I can to practice, but I don't want to miss a moment of enjoying my summer either. Who knows when I'll see her again? Hopefully soon, but I can't guarantee that.

~ ~ ~

Duncan has another date planned for us. I'm sure he spends all the time he isn't studying or rehearsing planning things for us to do. Not that I'm complaining, I love him for it.

He comes to my room after dinner to pick me up. He still doesn't tell me where we're going or what we are doing. I am glad I brought a cardigan to wear over my dress because we are walking there. We walk along the Thames holding hands. The water is still and there are few people out. Over on the other side of the water I can see St. Paul's cathedral lit up. I think I like this city better at night than I do in the day time.

"Do I get to know where we're going yet?" I ask.

"Nope. And don't try to guess, I won't be telling you if you're right or wrong."

Duncan interlaces his fingers through mine when we begin walking down the South bank. And elderly couple with matching khaki pants and black button down shirts smile up at us from the bench they're sitting on.

"We're going on the Eye again? I had fun the first time but we've already done that."

"You saw it in the morning. That's nothing compared to how it looks at night." The sun is just setting now so we get to see it with the hues of pink, orange, and yellow on the way up and we got to see it in total darkness on the way down. I'm able to see more stars than I expected since I've been in the city. All in all it was the perfect way to say goodbye to the summer. This time when we're in the glass pod in the sky, he has his arms wrapped around my waist and his head propped up on my shoulder. We're the only ones in the pod, so it feels like it's just us flying over London. I wish I could stay here forever.

We got off and started walking back.

"So how did you like it?"

"I loved it. I love this city. I don't want to leave."

"Wait, we need to do one more thing before you leave." He says and starts walking in the other direction. It takes a moment before I realize where he is going. He's going to the sidewalk where we first met. We get there and I sit down. He sets up his handheld camera on a rock across from us and put it on an auto capture setting and we posed for a couple photos. My favourite is the one with his hand intertwined in mine and my head on his shoulder with both of our eyes closed.

~ ~ ~

We're approaching the last couple of days of rehearsals and I am bouncing off the walls. Jenna is coming to visit me.

"Today's the big day, I can't wait to meet your friend," Tiana says at breakfast.

"Me too. She sounds awesome," James says.

"She totally needs this vacation after the breakup. I already got her tickets to our show. She's so excited to see her first play here. I know you guys are going to love her."

"I'm so excited to be here and to see you perform, you're going to be amazing. I bet you're going to win the award for best performance," she says excitedly.

"What do you want to do first while you're here?" I ask Jenna when she gets in to the room.

"So much, and I'm only here for a little while. There's this super cute cafe not far from here that I want to visit again, oh and I need to go shopping with Tiana , you've said so much about her and she seems like my soul mate. Have you even bought anything besides books now that you've been here?"

"Not really, I haven't had time to."

"We'll tomorrow we're taking you shopping."

"You are aware that the performance is only in a couple of days, right?"

"Yes I know that. And from what I understand you still have a couple pieces of your costume that you need to get after that Fleur bitch tried to destroy you."

"We should probably go today just to make sure we have time to find everything we need. I was meaning to find something to go with my dress. I haven't found the jewelry to go with it yet. We'll go right when Tiana gets home. Have you spoken to Steven or Max lately?"

"A little bit. He kind of wants to get back with me now. I still have feelings for him and I can't deny that. But I don't see why we would get back together. The problems we had while we were together will still be there now. I can't waste my time on someone I'm so different from."

"That's true," I say.

"Please don't tell me you still like Max."

"I don't. I'm with Duncan now and he's what's best for me."

"Are you guys going to try to make it work long distance?"

"Yes. I think we can do it."

"What if it's too hard?"

"Then we'll have to let it go. But I have faith in us."

Tiana comes home, looking exhausted, and slumps down on her bed and drops her binders down.

"I'm so sick of studying," she says and pouts. Just then, she notices Jenna and lets out a squeal, and jumps up to hug her.

"We're planning a shopping trip," Jenna says to Tiana , "we have to get Olivia some cute stuff while we're all here. You look tired, but we need your assistance."

"Never too tired to shop!" Tiana says and starts getting ready.

"Thank god you're going to get this girl something cute to wear. I've been nagging her all summer but she refused to change out of the jeans and t-shirt uniform." Tiana says.

"I know, right?"

"Anyway, so I was thinking..." Tiana and Jenna start excitedly walking ahead of me. I am still following them, and actually kind of excited to get something new, but I want to walk to Oxford Street slowly. I know I will be leaving soon and I love this city. I want to stay and enjoy it for as long as I can.

Jenna insists we take her to the costume store where we pick up our outfits for the performance. Normally we wouldn't be allowed in without a teacher supervising us but the owners knew Tiana well so they let us in. I never would have expected Jenna to find someone she was so similar to, especially in the way she dressed. She's in costume pretty much every day so I wouldn't be surprised if she bought one of these replica corsets to wear to work or something. She ends up leaving with some big, sparkly pieces of jewellery and a subtle, yet somehow still over the top, floor length black dress with shiny gold detailing on the bodice. She says she wants to wear it to the performance.

"Someone is going to think you're one of the actors."

"Maybe I should be. I am going to look more fabulous than half the people on stage," she says with a hair flick.

We also go to Primark and gets a few things, but Jenna insists I get some higher end things as well. I have spent surprisingly little over the course of my trip, considering how many lattes I've bought at The Muse, so I can afford it. I pick up a pair of light brown oxford shoes and a navy blue dress with a peter pan collar and instead of polka dots there is commas for a print. I know I have to have the book related dress, and Jenna and Tiana love the way it looks on me. Duncan and I are to go on a last date after the performance so now I have something to wear. I also pick up a big, blue bow hair clip to keep my bangs out of my face.

I'm done but Jenna and Tiana insisted we stop at a couple more antique stores to look and see if they have any jewellery she could do something with. Of course they do and she leaves with way more brushed silver pieces than she probably should have. While we were out shopping I decide I need to pick something up for Duncan that I can give him before I left. I'm not sure yet what that will be so I just continue looking around and hoped something would jump out at me.

I go in to a sporting goods store hoping there was something Duncan would like hat he doesn't already have.

"You're aware he has everything with the Chelsea logo on it, right?" Tiana says

"There must be *something* he doesn't have."

"You saw his room. He has everything, James told me. I think you should try to think outside the box with this one."

Later that evening, I settle in to the Muse with a copy of *Pride and Prejudice* I got here a week ago. I've ever read a Jane Austen book before, and I figured it was a good time to try it while I'm in England. As I sit down, a book on the shelf next to me catches my eye. It's a worn brown fabric-bound copy of *The Princess Bride*. The pages are yellowed but in good condition. It looks to be a first or special edition copy because it looks so nice and well taken care of. I remember my Mom reading this to be when I was younger. And suddenly, I realize who this is perfect for.

Chapter Twenty Two

Love is a smoke made with the fume of sighs -
Romeo and Juliet, William Shakespeare

    Today is the day. We are finally going to perform *The Merchant of Venice*. Everyone gets up at 6 AM and is buzzing around. I'm nervous but I force myself to eat an apple pancake and a glass of milk. It doesn't sit right so I only get through half of it before I have to leave. I pace the room reciting my lines.
    "WHERE IS MY EYELASH GLUE?" I hear Tiana yell from the bathroom.

"Don't they supply the makeup we wear?" I ask.
"YES, BUT THAT STUFF IS CRAP. I NEED MY OWN. AHH, I HAVE IT. CRISIS AVERTED." I'm not convinced we're facing a crisis but I don't correct her. Instead, I go up to Duncan's room.
"Hey, Sweetie. How you feeling?"
"Honestly, nervous as hell," I say.
"I know, but you'll be okay. We've practiced this like crazy. You could do this in your sleep."
"And I don't even have that big of a role. I'm acting crazy."
"You're not crazy, this is your first performance. You'll be nervous but you'll survive."
"How are you not scared?"
He shrugs. I've never really gotten nervous about this kind of stuff.
"Lucky bastard." I laugh.
"There we go, that's the laugh I was looking for. I've missed hearing that." He gives me a kiss. It makes me feel better. I'm not sure what I am going to do when I'm at home and don't have him to help me feel better.

It is time to get going to the theatre and getting ready. I see Tiana carrying bags of makeup and heaps of clothing down the hallway. Duncan and I take some of it from her and help her take it down.

"How are you feeling?" She asks, "a little cuddle with your boyfriend help make it all better?"
"Yes, actually," I say.
"My cuddles could make world peace," Duncan says, "of course it made her feel better. Besides, she has nothing to worry about."

"Ever feel like someone's talking about you like you're not there?" I say sarcastically. Duncan kisses me.

We arrive at the theatre and go backstage. Everyone is running around in the space around us. The the untrained eye it would look like chaos, but to everyone involved it is a well choreographed routine.

"WHERE ARE MY HAIR AND MAKEUP LADIES?" Marcus says, "AH, Tiana ! THERE YOU ARE. MY LOVE. NOW GET TO WORK." Apparently Marcus is going to yell at us all day. I'm not surprised he has to considering how loud it is back here, everyone trying to speak over each other to recite their lines and shout orders at people who didn't know what they are doing.

It's time for my scene with Duncan. I take a deep breath and walk onto stage on my cue.

SHYLOCK
What says that fool of Hagar's offspring, ha?
JESSICA
His words were 'Farewell mistress;' nothing else.
SHYLOCK
The patch is kind enough, but a huge feeder;
Snail-slow in profit, and he sleeps by day
More than the wild-cat: drones hive not with me;
Therefore I part with him, and part with him
To one that would have him help to waste
His borrow'd purse. Well, Jessica, go in;
Perhaps I will return immediately:
Do as I bid you; shut doors after you:
Fast bind, fast find;
A proverb never stale in thrifty mind.

Exit

JESSICA
Farewell; and if my fortune be not crost,
I have a father, you a daughter, lost.

> I walk off stage and he is waiting for me. He gives me a big bear hug and a kiss.
> "I am so proud of you," he says.
> "Thank you. I know you have more to perform so I'm going to wait by the others." He has to wait behind the curtain. I take a seat next to Tiana at the makeup mirrors. Her job is basically done but she sat nearby waiting for us to finish just in case there is an emergency. I stop talking to Tiana when I hear it is another of Duncan's scenes.

SHYLOCK
Why, there, there, there, there! a diamond gone,
cost me two thousand ducats in Frankfort! The curse
never fell upon our nation till now; I never felt it
till now: two thousand ducats in that; and other
precious, precious jewels. I would my daughter
were dead at my foot, and the jewels in her ear!
would she were hearsed at my foot, and the ducats in
her coffin! No news of them? Why, so: and I know
not what's spent in the search: why, thou loss upon
loss! the thief gone with so much, and so much to
find the thief; and no satisfaction, no revenge:
nor no in luck stirring but what lights on my
shoulders; no sighs but of my breathing; no tears
but of my shedding.
TUBAL

Yes, other men have ill luck too: Antonio, as I heard in Genoa,--
SHYLOCK
What, what, what? ill luck, ill luck?
TUBAL
Hath an argosy cast away, coming from Tripolis.
SHYLOCK
I thank God, I thank God. Is't true, is't true?

    He's doing so well, just like I knew he would be.

    The performance ends and we wait for the patrons to clear out of the building, and Jenna manages to sneak backstage and congratulate me. She can't stay for long as the winner of the contract would be announced soon, so she agrees to meet us at The Crown, where we'll be celebrating after the performance.

    We all sit on the benches and watch Marcus walk across the stage. I hold Duncan's hand.

    "I just wanted to congratulate you all for the wonderful job tonight. It was hard to pick a winner because everyone did so well. This was a long summer. We had a lot of good times, and some not so good. I feel my face turn red and Duncan squeeze my hand. I had to remind myself that the director quit and it was not my fault. I knew he was likely going to be fired, but even if that happened, he deserved it. What he did was wrong and I did the right thing by bringing it to the attention of the other people who work here. I did something good this summer. He won't victimize another student.

"With that being said, I would like to give this contract to James Smith for his wonderful performance." The crowd erupts into applause. Duncan, Harper, Tiana and I jump up and cheer. No one more than Tiana, though. He's going to spend another summer here with her.

Everyone's pleased with the outcome of the performance. No one messed up their lines or got so nervous they tossed their cookies on stage, which is a plus. We know we all did a good job and everyone loved James so it made it easier for them to not win it. We were all a little afraid they would give it to Fleur. Everyone knows what happened with her and Mr. Barnes by now. It's obvious now that everything with her and the corruption in this production was over now. Now we just have a week to relax and have a good time, and my best friend is still here for another three days. It's going to be a good week.

We all celebrate by going out to The Crown and buying way too much beer for James.

"My sexy professional actor," Tiana swings her arms around him and kisses him on the cheek. She's also had her fair share of cider so she slurs her words.

Fleur walks over to us and we all stop talking.

"Um… I just wanted to say good job. You worked hard. You deserve it," she says.

"Thanks, Fleur. I really appreciate it," he looks over at the bartender.

"Can I get a cider over here?" He asks, "you worked hard and did a great job, too. You deserve it." Fleur looked stunned. Tiana smiles proudly, knowing her boyfriend is a great guy. She's really lucky to have him. I motion to Fleur that I want to talk to her away from everyone else.

"I came here to talk to James, not you," she says.

"I know. Look, we started on really bad terms this year. I'm sorry it turned out that way. She'll never admit it, but I know Tiana kind of misses being friends with you. How about a truce?" I ask.

"Why?"

"You were friends with Tiana for years. I know you secretly care about her. Come have drinks with us. I know it would mean a lot to her."

"Fine," Fleur says, "for Tiana."

We return to our friends and I order a round of drinks for everyone.

So there I am, having a drink with the girl that kind of tried to destroy my relationship and career this summer. But hey, I don't tend to hold grudges so I finish my drink and challenge her to a game of darts. She wins by a landslide.

~ ~ ~

We have one weekend left before I have to go back to Canada, so Duncan planned out a last date for us. I put on the dress and shoes I bought when I was shopping with Jenna and Tiana, and Tiana curls my hair into soft waves. She puts on some concealer over my acne spots and a little blush on my cheeks and some natural looking lipstick. I must admit I look pretty good.

When we comes to pick me up, I opens the door and my heart skips a beat. He looks amazing. He rarely does anything with his hair, but tonight he decided to put in some gel and style it up a little. He's wearing a well-tailored navy suit and a white dress shirt and a black bow-tie. He has his black leather messenger bag, as usual. I am glad I dressed up a little because the place he was bringing me must be nice.

"You look… amazing," he says.

"I could say the same about yourself," I reply as he reaches for my hand.

He has one of those little black taxis waiting for us when we go down to the ground floor of the campus. He opens the door for me and I get in and slide over, and he soon follows.

He tells the taxi driver the name of the restaurant, Banquo. here. It's a short drive so we arrive pretty soon. The place doesn't look like much from the outside. It's in a long brick building, with many other restaurants and boutique shopping places around it. We go in and he tells the lady working at the front desk he has a reservation for two. She guides us through the restaurant and to a booth by the window on the far side of the restaurant.

The place is beautiful. It is dark but there are candles lit on all the tables, the tea lights are floating in a little dish filled with water. The waiter brings over the menus and Duncan orders a bottle of Chardonnay to start us off. I look at the menu and it is mainly Italian words I didn't know.

"How about we do something different today?" I ask.

"Do you not like the place?" He asks with a frightened look on his face.

"No, I didn't mean leave. Do you want to try to order for me? I think it would be fun."

"You can't read the menu, can you?" He laughs.

"On what planet do I read Italian?" I say, unimpressed.

"Okay, no problem." The waiter comes over and he orders both our meals. I realize I really trust him. I normally take food pretty seriously so I guess this means that I trust him more than I thought I would. If the meal comes out and I don't like it I think it would change my opinion of this guy.

The meals come out and I'm right to have trusted him. First there is garlic butter and cheese stuffed mushroom caps which are flawless. And then the best Caesar salad I've ever had in my life. The main course comes out and he has ordered pasta with a marinara sauce and it had scallops, mussels, and shrimp throughout. It has been so long since I've had shellfish. He knows it is something I had all the time at home because my Grandfather is a fisherman. He orders another bottle of Chardonnay.

"Oh I have something for you," he says when we were ordering desert. He reaches into his bag and pulls out a wrapped gift and hands it to me.

"You really didn't need to get me anything," I say.

"I know, now open it," he smiles.

I do. It's a pocket-sized blue umbrella.

"I mean I knew you would need another one at some point in time. And I didn't want you to go around getting rained on and meeting some other guy while you're in Canada, so now you have your own and you don't need to borrow anyone else's." Tears well up in my eyes. This is one of the most thoughtful things anyone has ever given me.

"I have something for you, too," I say. I reach into my purse and pull out a package wrapped in brown paper.

He unties the bow tied twine and the paper falls away from the book. I see him turn it over in his hands and read the back.

"This is perfect. I've wanted to read this forever."

"I found it at the Muse not long ago. I read it growing up. Buttercup and Westley are like, the best couple ever," I say. He puts the book on the seat next to him as our desert comes out and he pours me another glass of wine.

~ ~ ~

Jenna and I go out to The Crown for her last night here. I am so glad to have her here. I really loved it here but I missed home. She grounds me and kept me sane most of the time.

"I'm glad things have pretty much worked out," she says.

"Yeah. Pretty much."

"I know you have to leave Duncan and that sucks, but you guys can make it work. I know you can."

"It didn't work out with Harper."

"You're not Harper . Things can be different."

"I guess so."

"You did so much this summer. You made amazing, lifelong friends, kicked some ass at the final performance, had a ton of fun and even stopped a nasty director from continuing to sexually harass his students. If you can do all that in a matter of three months I can't wait to see how you and Duncan can make this distance seem like nothing in comparison."

"Thank you. Thank you so much," I say as I give her a hug. We talk for a little longer before it was time to get her suitcases and call a taxi, her Dad is getting ready for take-off soon.

It comes time to pack my bags and get ready to go to the airport. The Globe hired a bus to take us all in. People are already beginning to load up their things so I quickly shove everything in my bag. I am glad Jenna made me take the books out of my bags before I left because it means I have room for the mounds of books I bought from The Muse and the couple of dresses I got from local boutiques. I take the snow globe of *A Midsummer Night's Dream* off my nightstand and carefully wrap it in a t-shirt to keep it safe. Tiana and I finish packing at the same time and begin rolling our suitcases down to the bus.

Duncan and I sit on the seat together, with Harper behind us and Tiana and James in the seat in front of us. Most of the other people around us are talking to each other loudly but I don't hear them. We don't say much to each other on the way there. We just hold hands and occasionally sneak a kiss.

It's finally time for me to leave. Duncan helps me pull my suitcases off the bus and walks with me through the airport. We all ride together in the bus to Heathrow but some people are taking a train to their hometowns, everyone else is going to different terminals in the airport. I give Tiana, Harper, and James a hug goodbye and wave to them as they go through security. It's still a couple of hours before I have to board the plane, and unlike my way here, I never want that plane to come. Duncan and I sit down on a bench and watch our friends go through security. It isn't long before they wave to us one last time and then disappear out of our line of vision. We sit there in silence, his arms around me, or a while. There isn't much to say. The time comes for me to leave. I give him a hug and try to hold it together.

"I love you," he whispers in my ear when we embrace.

"I love you, too," we kiss for the last time before I have to get on the plane.

I go through security just in time for the final boarding. I brought a book with me but don't touch it the whole way home. I take a couple of tablets of melatonin and fall asleep right away. I know it won't be a good flight if I have to stay awake for it.

The plane lands and I wait in my seat until the rest of the plane empties out. I'm the last one on when I take my bag out of the overhead compartment and begin walking down the aisle. I see my parents as soon as I pick up my bag. They are beyond excited to see me and give me a big hug when they see me.

"I'm so glad to have you home. You got off the very last, I almost began to worry," Mom says. She's chronically anxious. I know this is not the first time she has worried this summer.

"Good to see you, Sweetie. Everyone is glad you're back. I went to Marlowe's the other day for lunch and Mildred says she can't wait for you to come back to work," Dad gives me a kiss on the cheek. I highly doubt that Mildred will be glad to see me, but I don't crush his way of trying to make me feel better.

"Where's John?" I ask.

"Oh, you know what he's like. He was sad you were gone for about five minutes and then promptly forgot you existed and got used to being an only child. We have to slowly reintegrate you into his life. If we can pull him away from his computer games to do so," Mom jokes.

    I sit in the backseat of Mom and Dad's car and get ready for the drive home. They insist I spend the weekend at home so I can share stories about my trip. I think they mostly want to take care of me and make sure I'm not falling apart without Duncan.

    I take out my phone and sent him a message.

    I'm home safe and I miss you. I love you.

He replies almost immediately.

    I'm been home for a while. Darcy is glad to see me. Mum and Dad are gone as usual. I still love you and miss you more than I thought I could miss anyone.

    I lean up against the window and buried my face in my arms, and cry despite myself. I never once thought I would cry over a boy, but I didn't know what love was before now and I most definitely did not know loss. I know he isn't gone forever but he is so far from me. I'm not sure I know how we make it through this distance.

Epilogue

All's well that ends well - All's Well That Ends Well, William Shakespeare

Duncan and I tried our hardest to stay together. It was hard at first. He still had a year left of his degree and I had three left. We did the long distance thing for a year. He was still in England and I was in Canada. He returned to the Globe on last summer but I couldn't join him. I couldn't renew my scholarship because it was only for entry level students. I couldn't afford the trip either. I could visit him once a year but the program fee was much too expensive and I needed to spend the summers working to help pay my regular tuition. There were many lonely nights but we made it work, we didn't have any other choice. After the year was up and he graduated he moved to Canada with me. Then it was hard for him because he missed his sister so much. She visited us a couple times though and we came back to England whenever we could. The best trip though was when we went there together, five years to the day that we met.

We get off the bus at Waterloo station because it is closest to the hotel he booked for us. It's drizzling that day, too. I shouldn't have been surprised because that's the standard weather but I've learned to like the rain more now. And blue umbrellas. After checking in to our campus and dropping off our things, we go for a walk. There is a showing of *Romeo and Juliet* tonight that I don't want to miss. We walk over to the stop where we met and sit down on the sidewalk. It has become a tradition to get a picture together every time we were there together. I hope to have many more in years to come. This is when he pulls a ring box out of his coat pocket and opens it up. I begin to feel tears welling up in my eyes. He didn't have to say anything. I knew what he was asking and I knew what my answer would be. He and I both know. We always knew. He puts the ring on my finger, still silent. Both of us crying. It is beautiful, that ring. It is white gold with a round diamond nestled between two small blue sapphires. It was perfect and so very much described us. We sit there for a minute before we decide to get up and go for a walk to the Globe. We see our show and hold hands the whole time. I can't wait to get home and call my family though.

When we do get back to the hotel and tell them they aren't surprised. He asked the ahead of time if he could ask me to marry him. Of course my parents said yes because they love him. He really is a great guy. We visit Darcy for a couple days on the trip and we already begin discussing wedding plans. I was sad that she and I wouldn't be in the same country for the planning but I still wanted her to be my maid of honour.

We end up having the ceremony in Canada because I had more family than he did.

We've met ten years ago to the day now. We came back to get another picture on Our Sidewalk – we've started calling it that. But this time our photo will have another addition to it. Belle, our daughter, is turning one soon.

Some people feel uneasy when they hear out daughter's name. Megan Bell is a huge part in who Duncan is and how he turned into the person I married. Her death is tragic but it matured him and made him realize how short life is and how much he didn't want to miss a moment of it. Without her being in his life he wouldn't be my husband. We both miss her, but I thank her for falling in love with him. If she didn't, neither would I. And that would mean our perfect daughter wouldn't be here either.

Acknowledgements

First and foremost, thank you to my parents Wayne Beaton and Cathy Warren for the unconditional love and support. My family, Brenda Beaton, Chris Warren, Jonathan Beaton, Cassie Williams, Bruce Williams, Ann (Bingo Nan) Williams, Kayla Mulrooney, Marcus Mulrooney, Denise Robertson, Kevin Roberston, and Jessica Robertson. I love all of you guys more than I could express. Scott, I love you with both my hearts. Sarah Croft and Jeanette Strebel for being my friends through the bouts of insanity that only those who are friends with writers know. Lisa Bartlett for being one of the best writer buddies ever. Hillary Frampton for being such honest and dependable beta reader. The teachers that have helped craft my love of literature: Robert Ormsby, Agnes Ormsby, Lisa Moore, Larry Mathews, Mary Dalton, Colleen Abbott, Krista Gregory. Colleen Hoover, for making me realize I'll never be as great a writer as you but also for giving me the courage to try. NaNoWriMo, for making me kill my inner editor for a whirl wind of 27 days that lead to this writing journey. The Newfoundland and Labrador Sexual Assault, Crisis, and Prevention Centre for helping me in my time of need. And, most importantly, to the readers. Thank you for supporting my writing, it means more than I could ever express to you.

Turn the page for an exclusive preview of my next novel, Christmas Mornings.

Coming Soon.

December 24, 1990

Rachel hated her parent's Christmas Eve parties.

"I can't believe you're making me do this again this year," Rachel said to her mother. Rachel scratched at the collar of her red dress. It was itchy and made her break out in hives if she wore it for too long. The velvet scratched up her arms and the white peter pan collar almost choked her. It was yet another gift from Aunt Penelope. She made nice designs but chose the worst fabric, so the dresses became the bane of every Christmas.

"You know the drill. Stand at the door and help us greet guests, do a round of shaking hands, and you can go back to your room and stick your nose in a stuffy book instead of having any fun. Do it with a smile and I'll pretend you didn't bring any of the wine into your room earlier," her mother replied.

The moments she had to spend at the parties were awful. It was full of aunts who pinched your cheeks, even if you're sixteen and you don't want them to, or people from work who always came in stuffy suits and far too fancy dresses. Rachel would stand with her parents by the door until everyone arrived, then she was free. She would try to sneak a glass of red wine into her room and have a plate toppling with crackers and her favourite cheeses. The people at the parties were boring but her parents knew what food to buy. Extra creamy brie heated to exactly the right temperature with homemade pesto and baked bread. There were huge slices of Applewood smoked cheddar. The best was the swiss. No one else liked swiss, but it was Rachel's favourite so she helped herself to half a plate full. Her Grandma Moore would have had a fit if she saw that. She was a movie star and model in the 50s which made her obsess over weight. Rachel had a few extra pounds that her Grandma sometimes commented on, but she could still run and fit into most of the cute clothes so her extra weight didn't bother her.

As the last few people trickled in, Rachel eyed the food table. She had already stowed one of the bottles of wine under her bed. Her parents knew she had an occasional drink. She said it was crucial to being a writer and eventually they stopped noticing or caring.

"Darling, there's someone here I would like you to meet," Rachel's father said. She turned and he was standing there with his hand on a boy's shoulder. The boy was cute. Tall and had brown hair that stood up in the front. It didn't look gelled though, it looked like it grew that way naturally. He had deep brown eyes and dark skin.

"Rachel," she said with her hand outstretched.

"Jesse," he replied. For some reason, this made her smile. It was awkward. His mother and her father were standing right there.

"Well..." Rachel said to break the silence, "it's nice to meet you." She took off towards the food table to continue with her plans for the night. When she got to her room and settled in on the window seat across from her bed she opened her book and began reading. She was finally having the night she imagined but she couldn't get her mind off of Jesse.

The hours ticked by and the party got louder. Rachel had fallen asleep on the window seat.

"Oh, shit, sorry," the door slammed and woke her up. She went out into the hallway to investigate what the hell that was.

"Sorry, I thought no one was in there," Jesse said.

"No, that's my room," Rachel replied.

"Yeah, I figured that out. It was just getting loud out here. Do you know of a place I can hang out until my parents are ready to leave?" he asked.

"You can come in here. I was just reading – well, I was sleeping, but before that I was reading – so it won't be that interesting but you can come anyway." She opened the door for him.

"So… this is my room," Rachel said and gestured around her. Then she decided that was dorky and stopped.

"It's nice," he said, looking at her bookshelf, "I appreciate the Nancy Drew but you need more Hardy Boys." The three bookshelves were filled to capacity. She had the whole original Nancy Drew series but only a handful of Hardy Boys.

"That's because they're lame. It takes one Nancy Drew to do what it takes two Hardy Boys to do. I could hardly get through the three I have," she said.

"Oh, ouch." Jesse held his hand against his heart in mock despair, "you know, I liked you, kid. Now I'm afraid we can never speak again." He sat down on the bed next to her. He smelled like aftershave, burnt wood, and Christmas cookies. "I'm so glad I don't have to go down there again. They were awful. My cheeks hurt."

"You have to learn how to avoid them. Clock in your half an hour greeting people and saying hi and enduring it for that long, and they you can be free. So why haven't I seen you at one of these parties before?"

"I'm new," Jesse said, popping a cracker into his mouth, "my Dad and your Dad work together. Dad just moved here for work and said yes to all the stupid holiday parties so he can get to know people and make connections. He's obsessed with getting a promotion, that's why we moved here. More room for upward mobility."

"What does he do at the company?"

"I don't know, like marketing or something. He travels a lot and does outreach things."

"I see."

"He's kind of starstruck to meet your Dad. With, you know, his position and all."

"He worked really hard to be CEO." Rachel was taken aback, and her response came out abrupt. He was making me her spoiled by having a Dad who was well off, but he didn't grow up that way.

"I know. But Dad is the child of first generation immigrants. He has high expectations for himself, just like everyone else had of him. He's a hard worker too, but he'll probably never make it to the top of the food chain. He'll try, though."

"Dad worked to put himself through business school. He was by far the most competent one in his class. But whatever, you don't want to hear about my family. I'm sure your Dad deserves the promotion. If I hear anything from Dad about promotions available, I can call you."

"Sure, here's my number." Rachel said.

"Great, thanks. So… I'll be here for a couple of hours. What do you want to do until then? Unless you want me to leave, which I can…"

"No, that's okay. I was reading before I fell asleep. I normally try to stay up late reading on Christmas Eve so I can wake up later on Christmas. We have to wait until after dinner to open presents. Family tradition." Rachel picked up the book on her bed and found the page she left off on. "You can take anything you want off my shelf. You can take it home, too. I'm sure we can arrange for me to get it back some other time."

"Sure. I'll try one of those Nancyyyy Drewwwww books if you insist they're so good," he drew out the words in a mocking tone.

"They are. You can read my favourite one. The classic, *The Secret of the Old Clock*."

"This is bullshit," Jesse said.

"Excuse me?"

"The book. It was good, but where is Ned, Bess, and George? They're the best characters in those books."

"So you *have* read some of them."

"Well, yeah. Just not all of them. Or in order."

"For your information, you are right, they are the best characters, but they weren't invented yet. I like the first one because it really started it all, you know? Those other characters don't come in until later."

"But they're so good! Why wouldn't the author want them in from the first book?"

"It's authors, actually. Carolyn Keene is a fake name. It's like eleven people who write them. One of them decided Nancy needed a boyfriend and some friends, so they wrote that in. Those books change all the time."

"Oh, I get it."

"Jesse!" They heard a woman's voice slur up the stairs.

"Mom's calling for me."

"The taxi's here!"

"Go to go! Bye, call me!" Jesse said before scurrying out the door, "oh, and Merry Christmas," he said, holding on to the doorframe and hanging in the room.

"Merry Christmas," Rachel said just before he left and pounded down the spiral staircase leading to the foyer.

"Good morning, Sweetie." Rachel's Mother said when she came down the stairs. She was still tired but knew she could take a nap later, but there was bacon sizzling on the stove top now."

"A latte, Rachel?"

"Just regular coffee please."

"That stuff smells so gross. And I have that nice machine that steams the milk, and I just bought some carmel syrup. I wish you would have something else. Or hot cocoa, I have that too…"

"Maybe later, Mom. While I'm reading. Thank you." She said when her Mother put the black coffee in front of her.

"So I heard you and Jesse spent some time together last night. I hope you were good."

"Mom," Rachel almost chocked on her hot coffee.

"I know, I know, so embarrassing. But really, you need to be safe. i know you won't be perfect, heck I wasn't at your age, but you need to be safe."

"I am, Mom. We ate crackers and read. That's all."

"Sure it is." Her Mother took a sip of her latte with a slight smile across her face.

Rachel loved her Mother. She was fun, and gave her more freedom than most of her friend's parents. Probably because Rachel's Grandparents were so strict. She hasn't spoken to them in years. Her Mom just had her sister Penelope and the family she created now.

"When can we open presents?" Rachel asked, eyeing the bottom of the tree overflowing with gifts.

"Not until after dinner at Grandma Moore's. You know the rules, dear. How do you want your eggs?"

"Scrambled with melted cheese on top, please."

"Good, morning, everyone!" Rachel's Dad said when he came down the stairs. He was dressed in his form of casual - ironed black pants with a dress shirt. he refused to wear his pyjamas outside of the bedroom, even at home on Christmas morning like a normal person.

"Breakfast is on the table, darling. Rachel has been eyeing the tree. I would keep an eye on that one."

"If she helps do the breakfast dishes, maybe she can open one early." Her Dad winked at her.

"Will do, after my run" Rachel had gone for a six mile jog every Christmas since she joined the track team. She tried to double her three mile run that she took on regular mornings, but she was never a cross country runner, always a sprinter. She put on her warmest clothes and her running shoes and started off.

"We can start opening presents now, if you want," her Dad said. She could tell there was one present in particular he wanted her to open. She was shocked to find the newest music player, a cassette tae based walkman, there for her.

"Dad, that's way too much," she said. Rachel had knit her parents each scarves, which they put on immediately. They were in horrifically bright coloured stripes, but Rachel liked the colours and thought neutrally toned clothes was far too boring. She liked to be bright as possible in neon.

"It's something special for you, you can take it out on your runs with you. I got some things to go with it." She continued to open the individually wrapped cassette tapes.

"Thank you so much," she embraced her Dad. They continued opening up gifts and, as per annual, tradition, had hot chocolate and each read a book in the living room.

"I heard you introduced Jesse to one of your favourite books yesterday," her Dad said when he put the three large marshmallows in her drink.

"I did. He needed to learn which books were worth reading."

"He's a nice boy, you know. His Dad is a hard worker. His Dad worked hard to move to America from India. You should see him more, I like him."

"Why do you like him so much?"

"You've never dated anyone. I guess I want to see you have fun. Be a teenage girl."

"Having a sixteen year old more interested in studying is most fathers dream. You should consider yourself lucky."

"I do, Rachel. Every day," her Dad said with a kiss on her cheek.

About the Author

Chelsea Bee was born in Ottawa, Ontario in 1993, and fell in love with books shortly after.

Beginning with chewing on them, she eventually learned to read and enjoyed that much more than eating books, though she still believes they smell quite nice.

Chelsea started writing when she was fourteen in the small town of Arnold's Cove, Newfoundland. The first book she attempted was awful and embarrassing, and she was glad that it was destroyed with her first laptop.

She gave up for many years, until 2014 while residing in St. John's, Newfoundland, when she decided three days before November that she would participate in National Novel Writing Month (NaNoWriMo). Chelsea didn't have a functioning computer at the time, so she wrote the entirety of what is now London Calling using the computers in the Memorial University Library after finishing her classes and part time job. She hasn't stopped writing or editing since.

She still hasn't caught up on her missed sleep.

Follow Chelsea on Facebook, Instagram, and Twitter @chelseabeebooks.

Made in the USA
Middletown, DE
20 August 2017